Immortal Ops:
RADAR DECEPTION

By

Mandy M. Roth

Paranormal Romance

New Concepts   Georgia

Be sure to check out our website for the very best in fiction at fantastic prices!

When you visit our webpage, you can:
* Read excerpts of currently available books
* View cover art of upcoming books and current releases
* Find out more about the talented artists who capture the magic of the writer's imagination on the covers
* Order books from our backlist
* Find out the latest NCP and author news--including any upcoming book signings by your favorite NCP author
* Read author bios and reviews of our books
* Get NCP submission guidelines
* And so much more!

We offer a 20% discount on all new Trade Paperback releases ordered from our website!

Be sure to visit our webpage to find the best deals in e-books and paperbacks! To find out about our new releases as soon as they are available, please be sure to sign up for our newsletter (http://www.newconceptspublishing.com/newsletter.htm) or join our reader group (http://groups.yahoo.com/group/new_concepts_pub/join)!

The newsletter is available by double opt in only and our customer information is *never* shared!

Visit our webpage at:
www.newconceptspublishing.com

Radar Deception is an original publication of NCP. This work has never before appeared in book form. This work is a novel. Any similarity to actual persons or events is purely coincidental.

New Concepts Publishing, Inc.
5202 Humphreys Rd.
Lake Park, GA 31636

ISBN 978-1-58608-897-2
© 2006 Mandy M. Roth
Cover art (c) copyright 2006 Eliza Black

All rights reserved, which includes the right to reproduce this book or portions thereof in any form whatsoever except as provided by the U.S. Copyright Law.

If you purchased this book without a cover you should be aware this book is stolen property.

NCP books are available at special quantity discounts for bulk purchases for sales promotions, premiums, fund raising, or educational use. For details, write, email, or phone New Concepts Publishing, Inc., 5202 Humphreys Rd., Lake Park, GA 31636; Ph. 229-257-0367, Fax 229-219-1097; orders@newconceptspublishing.com.

First NCP Trade Paperback Printing: March 2007

Dedication:

To Shane, my sexy hero who also happens to be a *bit* of a science geek. It's okay, honey, so long as you're not against me in trivia again. How is it you seem to know the answer to every question? I love you.

Radar Deception

The deliberate radiation, re-radiation, alteration, suppression, absorption, denial, enhancement, or reflection of electromagnetic energy in a manner intended to convey misleading information to an enemy or to enemy electromagnetic-dependent weapons, thereby degrading or neutralizing the enemy's combat capability. Among the types of electromagnetic deception are: a. manipulative electromagnetic deception--Actions to eliminate revealing, or convey misleading, electromagnetic telltale indicators that may be used by hostile forces; b. simulative electromagnetic deception--Actions to simulate friendly, notional, or actual capabilities to mislead hostile forces; and c. imitative electromagnetic deception--The introduction of electromagnetic energy into enemy systems that imitates enemy emissions. ~ *Department of Defense Dictionary of Military and Associated Terms*

Prologue

Melanie sat--bordering on catatonic--as her best friends tried to comfort her. Their night had been anything but ordinary. What had been planned as a birthday outing for her friend Peren quickly turned bizarre, dark and deadly. It had been her idea to drag Peren out and about--get her back in the land of the living since she'd taken to locking herself away from mankind.

Missy, her other close friend, agreed and the two plotted a way to get Peren on a date. It had taken some work on their part and after a few phone calls, Missy had set up what Melanie had assumed was a fool-proof night. Well, right up until Peren bolted from the bar and Lukian, the man set up to be her blind date, went after her, leaving Missy and Melanie being shoved into an unmarked van by two armed hunks.

Once Lance and Roi, the two hunks, had explained that Peren was in danger and that they were there to help, she'd calmed down a bit. Missy, the hellcat that she was, didn't let up once. She'd even gone as far as to smack Roi across the face and then spend the remainder of the evening arguing with him.

Melanie hadn't used her head. No. She'd followed blindly behind Lance, seemingly unable to deny the simplest of his requests. Something about him left her feeling as if she had no choice but to comply. She also hadn't been able to tear her gaze from him. When he'd come onto her, rubbing, petting, kissing, it felt right but wrong for reasons she couldn't name. Still, she gave in, letting him please her multiple times. It wasn't until their third time joining that it happened.

Melanie shuddered as she sat in the cold steel chair. The light in the room was harsh and the room itself had a vibe to it, reminding her of integration rooms on television shows.

"Mel, guess what our little buddy did," Missy said, folding her arms over her chest and arching a dark brown towards their friend Peren.

Still too distracted by the night's event to fully focus on whatever had set Missy off this time, Melanie looked at Peren. "What'd ya' do?"

"Mel?"

"What's wrong, honey?" Peren asked, concern lacing her voice.

The feel of being watched came over Melanie but she shrugged it off, doing her best to concentrate on her friends. "I ... I had sex with Lance last night."

Missy grunted and Peren shot her a nasty look.

Melanie continued on, "He was just ... I mean, well, he wasn't...oh, shit, he was hot and I wanted him." Shame filling her, she glanced at Peren. "I got him. I got more than just him. We fucked three times before *it* happened." She took a keen interest in the floor, wanting to avoid her friends' stare. "You won't believe me if I tell you."

"No, sweetie, it's okay. We'll believe you, go ahead," Peren said, moving closer.

Melanie took her friend's hand and held it tight. "You're going to think I'm crazy, but I swear to you ... Lance changed during his orgasm."

"Changed?" Peren asked, rubbing her thumb over the back of Melanie's hand.

Missy snorted and rolled her eyes. "Yeah, psycho-paramilitary freaks tend to do that."

"He changed how?" Peren asked.

Melanie debated on ending the discussion then and there. It was bad enough she was sure she'd lost her mind seeing the impossible, but to share her insanity with her friends was another matter. Peren gave her hand a gentle tug, reassuring her.

Melanie nodded more to herself than anyone else. "His mouth widened and then his shoulders moved up ... hair, dark black hair just sort of appeared all over him, and the worst part was his teeth ... they were huge ... he looked like," she gasped, "he looked like he was going tear me apart after he fucked me."

"Oh, this is ridiculous!" Missy stood quickly, tipping her chair over. "He obviously slipped you something in your drink at the club and you were hallucinating."

Melanie wiped the tears from her cheeks, embarrassed and humiliated by what she'd said--what she'd done. "Hallucinating? Yeah, maybe, but it felt ... it felt so real."

It was real.

Inside she knew, but she didn't voice it aloud. There was no point. No one believed her.

Missy gave a rather dramatic wave with her hand while she huffed. "Well, you don't have a mark on you and since you're sitting here telling us this, he couldn't have eaten you."

"Yeah, yeah, you're right," Melanie said, knowing to just play along rather than make any more waves. "When I got up this morning he was lying next to me in the bed, normal. I ... yeah, it must have been something in my drink."

Peren held her tight. "Yes, you were tired, and had too much to drink. Lance didn't slip you a thing. You were half in the bag when we got to the club, and you've been running on empty with finals lately. I'm guessing that the stress of all that, combined with alcohol, left you a little off."

Melanie didn't believe Peren was as sure as she presented herself to be. In fact, Melanie's powers, the ones she kept hidden from her friends, told her that Peren was as worried about Melanie's revelation as she was. Maybe more.

She waited until Peren glanced away to close her eyes and try to calm her nerves. Someone's rage swept over her and for a split second she could have sworn she heard the auburn-haired man's voice--the one who had driven the van away after Lance told her to get in. The one whose emerald eyes locked on her in the review mirror and rarely left. The one who made her feel uncomfortable but not in a bad way. What had Lance called him?

Green.

That's right.

Green.

Melanie stared around the white room. She, Missy and Peren were the only ones in it. Still, she couldn't shake the feeling she was being watched. Her gaze flickered to the mirror, running the full length of the left-hand wall.

Drawing upon her power, she let the tiniest bit out and watched in awe as Green lunged at a man she didn't recognize. Green paused and looked in her direction, as if he felt her gaze on him.

Melanie stiffened and dropped her power quickly. Peren wrapped her arms around her and gave her a gentle squeeze. "It's okay, Mel."

"Thanks," she said, holding tight, still thinking about Green when she should be thinking about Lance.

Chapter One

Two and a half weeks later....

"Brava, this is Alpha Dog Two, do you have a lock on the target? I repeat--do you have a lock?" The sound of Roi Major's voice filled Green's earpiece as he swiveled around in his chair to check the secondary computer monitors. The liquid crystal display and drop-down ability certainly cleaned up much needed counter area in the surveillance van. The days of turning and accidentally putting his elbow through a monitor that was as big--if not bigger than--some televisions were long gone. Now, with his supernatural strength, he only put his elbow through the machines when not paying attention.

Much better.

The interior of the van was still cramped for a man of his size but he was used to it so he didn't complain. The line feeding into the monitors was from the inner dwellings of the nearest known hotspot for the enemy. It was a lab specializing in genetic research and development. In the grander scale of things, the lab was a small one but it needed to be destroyed all the same.

Gisbert Krauss, the team's main focus of the moment, had been funneling money throughout Europe and Asia for the last thirty years. His fascination with the idea of immortality and power put the scientist in the forefront of genetic research. Publications in the area of genetics claimed that Krauss was on the verge of some sort of genetic breakthrough. Intel gathered on him proved that he wasn't just on the threshold of something big, he'd already succeeded and had been conducting research on humans for decades. He'd even been daring enough to have an underground paranormal website talking about DNA alterations and the making of super humans with the potential to be used as weapons for the highest paying governments. A paper trail connected Krauss with Pierre Molyneux, a master vampire who was legendary throughout the supernatural community as a man with means and a wicked bad side. With Molyneux's connections, Krauss could transport just about anything between countries under the guise of it being art. In the case of Krauss, he was no doubt transporting human cargo and who knew what else.

Green knew after having been briefed by Colonel Brooks on Intel's latest findings that Krauss had been behind assembling a large group of women in Asia from around the world, impregnating and experimenting on their children *in utero*. The mothers of the children disappeared once they were born. The more likely explanation was that the mothers were murdered. Apparently, the enemy had aborted their project, or rather hid their testing better because I-Ops got a little too close to discovering them.

The enemy spread the surviving children out to orphanages in various countries. Most were third-world, but from the data Green had read, some were dumped in the United States as well. The majority of their experiments on fetuses and newborns took place between twenty to thirty years ago. The *Asia Project* was massive. Green had initially assumed the children would not have survived, that they would have died when their bodies attempted a shift or that they'd have gone insane long ago. He'd been wrong. Records indicated that all of them had indeed made it to adulthood. He couldn't fathom how they coped with having enhanced abilities and turning into an animal or a vampire without warning. It had to leave some sort of lasting damage.

The main issue at hand was that Krauss' people were sacrificing innocent lives in the name of science and attempting to round up the children from the *Asia Project*. Green didn't want to think about what would happen should Krauss get his hands on the people who had once been subjected to testing unwillingly. The very fact that these children managed to grow to be adults spoke volumes about their will to live. Krauss had to know that and he'd exploit it for all it was worth. If that wasn't enough, information was trickling in that Krauss may have aligned with a powerful Fae.

Shuddering at the thought, Green rubbed his temple. Almost instantly, images of Melanie, a Fae and sister to Eadan, the newest member of the I-Ops team, flooded his mind. She was still clueless as to whom they were and their relationship to one another--thinking her friends were merely girlfriends to I-Ops members when in reality they were now lifemates, spouses.

His cock hardened and his pulse raced. Melanie had worked her way under his defenses and left her imprint. Already he'd spent many a night stroking himself to peak, guided by thoughts of her. Her blue eyes. Her long, white-blonde hair. Her seemingly endless legs. Her scent-- distinctly feminine and familiar to him. He needed to touch her and soon or risk going insane. Or developing carpal tunnel from excessive masturbation.

"Bravo Dog One, do we have a go?" Roi asked, drawing Green from his thoughts of Melanie.

Green punched in the sequence of numbers needed to access the facility's computer system and waited for confirmation that he was indeed in. It had been a bit trickier than he'd assumed it would be to hack into Krauss' facility but he was confident of his skills.

When a map of the building's blueprints popped up and an analysis of the security system displayed, he smiled. "Alpha Dog Two, you have a 'go' to enter. Once in, you will find two, I repeat, two, tangos. There is a four-second window until my hacks will open the main gate from there. If you attempt to force it, you will set off secondary alarms. Do you read?"

"Copy that. Get antsy and bad things will happen," Roi said, being his normal sardonic self. He was also famous for simplifying things. As usual, he held true to expectations. "We'll kill 'em quietly and then wait for the 'magik doors' to open. Do we have to say 'open sesame' or do you think your mega brain got the calculations right?"

Captain Lukian Vlakhusha sighed into his headset, clearly annoyed with Roi. It was normal, so no one commented. Besides, they were like brothers. If Roi got too obnoxious, Lukian would just slap him. Arching a brow, Green hoped Lukian might actually haul off and hit Roi. Then again, it could damage the equipment Roi had on. Green had always been partial to technology, though Roi wasn't too bad either.

Decisions. Decisions.

Green watched the other monitors--there were six in all. Each displayed images of the team members. The cameras were mounted to their headgear. Each soldier was equipped with a small flip visor that when in place, covered one of their eyes. If on, the person could see what a selected team member was viewing. While disengaged, they merely looked through a slightly tinted eye-piece. Green, on the other hand, was able to view what each one of them was currently seeing. It was a little like being a god, at least according to Roi.

Lukian, his captain, was with Roi waiting to enter through the west entrance. Wilson and Eadan were near the south end of the facility, awaiting orders to move in and assist if need be. Jon, the team sniper, was stationed on the north tower, having already taken out the two guards with the hope for more kills. His location was perfect to provide cover should things go awry. The other two monitors provided visuals from Peren, Lukian's wife and lifemate, and Missy, Roi's wife and lifemate.

The women were in a secure location three miles up the road in another van, watching the feed from Green's van. Missy had only just found out she was expecting a child and no one wanted her to go in with the men, regardless of how qualified she was. Missy was a level-one agent with Paranormal Security and Intelligence (PSI). PSI was basically the CIA of the supernatural community. Since humans weren't permitted to have the knowledge that supernaturals existed, the government denied any and all knowledge of PSI's existence. Since Missy had also been experimented on in the *Asia Project*, she had a personal stake in the matter at hand.

Green hated Krauss for playing God but even he had to admire the man's genius. Krauss had managed to introduce small quantities of supernatural DNA into the bloodstream of an adult human without killing them. That was all but unheard of. Somehow, Green and the men he'd originally worked for had gotten lucky enough to do something similar during the Immortal Ops inception. Each man, with the exception of Green and Lukian, had been injected with DNA to alter their own. They survived. No others had. The good guys stopped trying to play God after that. The bad guys took it as a cue to what was possible and as a sign to proceed.

Krauss' strands of DNA and his testing increased a person's physical strength but did not permit them to be able to shift forms or be immortal. That did set his experiments and those subjected to them apart from the I-Ops, who could indeed fully shift and were technically immortal.

Krauss had found a way to enhance those who were already supernatural. This eluded I-Ops. Basically, Krauss had managed to introduce other aspects of supernaturals into a pre-existing one. Meaning, he could, theoretically, give a vampire similar traits as a werewolf. All and all, Krauss could and would be powerful enough to take down even the I-Ops at the rate he was going. He was a new kind of evil. One who would stop at nothing to rule the world.

Green twisted in his seat once more, keying in the coordinates to the satellite above. It took a second but it synced up and began systematically zooming in as per his instructions, generating 3-D images of the area as it went. The images showed the facility, his van, the second van containing Peren and Missy, and the surrounding area. The moment he spotted vehicles that weren't supposed to be there, he let out a long breath.

Of course. Nothing can be easy.

Glancing at the screen for Jon, Green estimated their "guests" arrival time. "Bravo Tiger Two, we've got a convoy of vehicles moving in from the north. ETA, two minutes."

"Copy that," Jon said, no doubt positioning himself to watch through his scope as the convoy approached. "I have a visual."

That didn't surprise Green. Jon was part were-tiger and had amazing eyesight to begin with. Add in the use of a scope and it was damn hard to fall out of his line of sight, making Green very happy they were on the same side considering how accurate Jon was within 4000 meters. Anything above that and Jon had to fight the limits of technology. He didn't have to fight his eyesight.

Green noted that Roi and Lukian had taken out the enemies within the entrance to the facility just in time for his hacks to begin to take effect. The gate opened a second after the Trojan horse Green had loaded into the system a few days prior began to work its magic, taking down the alarms in alternate locations to avoid raising suspicions.

"How are our boys doing?" Peren asked, over her intercom link to Green.

It was easy to pick up how nervous she was and Green was thankful he'd thought to keep the girls off the team's main line of communication. He didn't need Lukian or Roi getting distracted by their mates' concerns. The women could hear the men just fine but until Green flipped another switch, only he could hear the women.

"Alpha Team, proceed to level two," he said, watching the facility's sensors for signs of life forms but finding none in the stairwell. "On your left will be the cryogenics room. On the right you'll find a mini-lab. From there, you'll see an operating room and according to PSI Intel, a room used to cage animals and humans. I'm not detecting any life forms at present. Proceed with caution."

"Alpha Team is a go," Lukian said.

Green watched silently as Lukian entered the room and planted charges. They would not allow any frozen embryos or other DNA material collected by Krauss' people to survive. As much as they all needed to fully understand DNA splicing and manipulation better, it wasn't worth the risk of it falling into enemy hands once more. Besides, I-Ops and PSI would never enter back into experiments that could cost lives. They'd learned their lesson long ago and had no intentions of allowing history to repeat itself.

Spinning in his chair, Green spotted another problem. "Shit!"

"Aww, I hate it when he says that," Wilson, resident smart ass and were-rat extraordinaire, said wryly.

Green ignored him, focusing instead on the three red dots moving down the corridor closest to Wilson and Eadan. "Bravo Rat Three, prepare to engage hostiles in three ... two ... one." The door nearest them opened and Green watched with bated breath as Wilson snapped one man's neck while Eadan, a full-blooded Fae, used his power to silently kill the other two.

Wilson stared at Eadan, his face filling the viewing screen before Green. "Ya think you could give us a bit more warning next time, Mr. Science Geek?"

Green rolled his eyes. "Cut the chatter, Rat."

Wilson flipped Green off. Green returned the favor even though he knew Wilson couldn't see it. He smiled. "You're lucky Eadan is with you or I'd have let you figure out on your own that the enemy was coming."

Eadan chuckled. "I appreciate that, Green. More than you know."

Wilson mumbled something about the fucking faerie getting more respect than him and then shut up. Green couldn't help but laugh. Double checking the satellite feed, he grunted. "Bravo Tiger Two, report."

"Tell me when they're done," Jon said quietly, always a sign he was concentrating on the target. His normally slight southern drawl always seemed to intensify when he stopped thinking about it. He also had a habit of asking his "momma" to forgive him every time he took a man out by way of sniper rifle. Green wasn't even sure Jon realized he did it, but all in all, it seemed to keep Jon real. The threat of losing touch with humanity was a danger for the I-Ops, one they hoped they'd never succumb to.

"Charges are in place," Lukian reported. "We need to move, now!"

Green nodded. "Alpha and Bravo Teams, pull out. I repeat, pull out. Charges are set."

A round of acknowledgements followed as Green kept his eyes on the monitors. He mentally began calculating the amount of time it would take each operative to make it back to the van and then how far they needed to be from the facility to assure a clear, safe distance before detonating the charges.

Lukian and Roi were the first ones to make it back to the van. Roi took the driver's seat and Lukian rode shotgun. Green thrust the back door open just in time for Jon to hop in. Glancing back at the monitors, Green spotted six red dots moving in on Wilson and Eadan's location.

"Bravo Rat Three, you've got company. Consider my warning an early Christmas present. Roi was planning on buying you cheese. See, my gift is better."

Wilson snorted and mumbled under his breath, "Asshole."

"How many?" Eadan asked as he ran next to Wilson. The view, projected out from tiny cameras attached near the bands wrapped around the back of their heads, shook. It was nauseating but Green had grown accustomed to it over the years. Jon looked away, clearly not as conditioned to watching the image shake.

"If you're planning on being sick, do me the courtesy of doing it outside of the van," Green said, smiling as Jon's face paled.

Jon nodded and then hopped out of the van. Green did his best to ignore the retching sound and concentrated on Wilson and Eadan's progress. Finding it halted, he shot a glance at Lukian. "Captain, they're pinned in."

"Jon!" Lukian yelled. "Get your ass in here. Roi, get us to that side of the building, now!"

"Yes, sir."

The van lurched forward, causing Green to fall against the control panel. He had a half a second to wonder what he might have turned on or off accidentally before he reacted. Green grabbed Jon just in time to pull him in before he'd have been left behind, and then exhaled loudly. "You okay?"

"Yeah," Jon said, his voice a bit off kilter. He patted himself once for good measure obviously not as confident in his answer as he'd have liked all to believe.

"Green, is everyone alive?" Missy asked, reminding him she was up the road waiting. "Are they okay? God, please tell me that Roi didn't do anything stupid."

"Hey! I heard that. And I'll have you know, dear wife, I never do anything stupid while on a mission." Roi chuckled as he took the van off road and through a six-foot metal fence. "Hot damn!"

It was then Green realized he must have opened the lines of communication to the women when he fell onto the control panel. Now wasn't the time to worry about it though. The van lifted off the ground again and slammed down, rocking its occupants violently. Equipment that was technically secure scattered about. Their weapons slid away only to be replaced by others.

Lukian smacked Roi upside the back of the head and growled. "Brother, you're going to get us killed!"

"Technically," Green said, leaning forward. "We're immortal, so unless you end up decapitated or something pierces your heart, you should live. Granted, there is always the chance I'm wrong."

Lukian arched a black brow and stared back at him. It was the one bearing a tiny scar he'd gotten when he was just a boy. Somehow, it had always made him seem more real to Green. "Not helping here, Green. Really."

"Sorry, Captain."

"Don't apologize. Just don't remind me how losing my head is a bad thing. At least not when I'm about to stick my neck on the line--literally." Laughing, Lukian leaned out of the window, his M4 Carbine in hand as he laid down cover fire. Wilson and Eadan were still pinned in. They wouldn't make it out in time with the convoy of men dispersing on the other side of the facility. Green grabbed a M203 Grenade Launcher from the weapons chest to his left, thankful it wasn't bouncing around the van as well, and handed it to Jon. "Open the back door and fire at the second level, fourth window in from the right." He glanced at Roi. "Roi, spin in a circle, now!"

"Yeehaw!" Roi yelled, taking his daredevil ways to a new level as he came close to overturning the van. It tipped, lifted off the wheels on one side before slamming back down and bouncing.

"Goddamnit, Major!" Jon snarled, still looking a bit pale.

"Roi, if you get yourself killed, I am never having sex with you again," Missy bit out over the headsets.

It was illogical but effective. Roi immediately began to behave himself. "Sorry, doll baby."

Jon thrust the back door open and aimed the weapon higher than need be to aid in the trajectory.

"Eadan, throw power around Wilson and yourself, now," Green said, calmly into his microphone, knowing the Fae could handle the request. "And I suggest you run now. Trust me when I say a bullet is better than a building falling on you."

"Tell him the head and heart story," Roi said, laughing under his breath. "That should make him feel much better about his odds."

A semi-growl like noise came from Missy.

"Shutting up now, dear," Roi whispered.

"Oh, shit!" Wilson and Eadan ran full force toward the van. Green grabbed an M-16 and immediately began laying down cover fire for them. Lukian leaned out his window and did the same. Jon hit his mark, as Green knew he would, and the grenade exploded. Eadan dove into the van, careful to stay under Green's line of fire. Wilson followed suit as something close to a sonic boom followed. Jon grabbed one door and Green grabbed the other, pulling them closed.

"Get us out of here, now!" Lukian shouted.

Roi chuckled "Oh, now you want my Andretti skills."

"Do not make me shoot you." The fake snarl from Lukian told them all he was joking.

Eadan lay on his back, laughing as they sped away. Flames engulfed the building, shooting out in all directions. Jon glanced down at Eadan. "Did you snap or do you always laugh when you come close to dying?"

It was Missy who answered. "He always does that. Give him about ten minutes. He'll snap out of it. I went from one hot dog to another." She would know how Eadan normally behaved. She'd been married to him years ago. Roi and Eadan had worked out their differences and had come to an understanding.

Roi huffed. "I am not a hot dog. More like a great big, I'm talking huge ... mongo even, sausage."

Everyone laughed. After dangerous missions when everyone made it out relatively unharmed, the men tended to rely on humor to keep their wits and their ties to something non-violent. For too many years they'd been the silent operatives, going in and eliminating targets the world wasn't even aware it had. It tended to wear on the human side of them while feeding their beasts.

Wilson tapped Green's leg. "Do me a favor and pull out the bullet in my shoulder I don't think it's in deep. I can probably have it healed by morning."

"Dare I guess how many bullets you'll take when we get to South America? You seem like a magnet."

Jon grinned. "I could use him for target practice now so he's good and conditioned."

"I want to help," Roi said, chuckling.

Lukian ignored their banter, pulling a chart out and flicking on his mini-flashlight instead. He was anal about the reports they filed with Colonel Brooks. Green had no doubt that Lukian would have the paperwork needed for the briefing done by the time the rest of them were home and showered.

Eadan nudged Wilson. "If it helps, I have no desire to shoot you--yet."

"*Gee*, I feel *so* much better now."

Eadan snickered. "Yeah, I thought that would make you feel better. I'm charming like that."

"Eadan, uhh, umm, never mind," Green muttered, unsure why thoughts of Melanie's well-being hit him out of nowhere.

The Fae glanced up at him and gave him a soft look. "Yes, Green. Melanie is still okay. I can sense her through our bond. I've never been able to pick up on her activities but when she's not consciously blocking me, I'm able to read her feelings. I'm guessing she's resting because its one of the only ways Melanie's mind relaxes enough not to fight back."

Exhaling, Green nodded. "Thank you."

"You know," Wilson arched a brow, "you could just call her. Ask her out on a date. Read from one of those boring science books. Talk about mating rituals of penguins or whatever else geeks like you enjoy. Anything."

"I will." As Green said it, he knew it was a lie. He'd never gather the courage to ask someone like Melanie out. She was so vibrant, so carefree, a woman he couldn't understand but couldn't get out of his mind either.

"Mmmhmm." The look on Wilson's face said he didn't believe for a second Green would call. He was right.

"Uhh, not to break up this 'feel good' moment," Jon pointed at the viewing screens, "but is that a guy on the corner of the guard shack with an RPG launcher?"

For a split second, no one said a word. The moment Jon lunged toward the weapons chest, everyone, including Roi, who was driving, reached for one. Lukian smacked him in the back of the head again. "Idiot, watch the road!"

"Oh, right."

The rest of the men armed themselves with something capable of shooting longer distances and went into action. Eadan sat up, lifted his hands and released his magik. It ran over Green, making the air around him buzz and the hair on his arm stand on end. The doors to the van burst open. Jon and Wilson began firing.

"Take out that RPG!" Lukian yelled as if they needed to be told something so obvious.

Green tapped Jon's shoulder. "Too high, you're over shooting."

"Ha, Mr. Science Geek thinks he can do better." Wilson fired as much as his mouth ran. That always left him going through ammo quicker than others.

Ignoring his comment, Green held his weapon, aimed, doing his best to mentally calculate the rate at which the vehicle was moving, versus the position of the man about to fire a rocket-propelled grenade at them, and fired. The man dropped as he fired the RPG. All of them watched in horror as a trail of fire seemed to streak towards them.

"Oh shit," Green whispered.

"See, when *he* says that," Wilson glanced at Green, "it's always bad."

"Nah." Roi chuckled, glancing in the review mirror. "That's going wide. It'll miss us by a--"

The RPG shot past the van, narrowly missing it and causing it to rock slightly. Roi looked at Lukian. "Umm, by a centimeter or two. See. All is fine. Anyone else impressed Green stepped up and nailed the guy with one shot?"

Putting his hand up, Green let out a soft laugh. "I am."

"Just another day at the office, buddy." Jon patted Green on the shoulder. "Nice shot."

"I'm getting too old for this shit."

"Aren't we all?"

Chapter Two

Melanie Daly leaned against the wall at the upscale club, listening to the sounds of various Rat Pack members piped through the speakers. It was a place she'd always loved coming to. Not so much for the food--that was good too--but the atmosphere was amazing. It looked like a Hollywood movie set with its high vaulted ceiling and silver, black and white walls. Art Deco was something she'd always had a thing for and this place had it in spades.

The dance floor was full of couples enjoying their evening and every ounce of Melanie wanted to go out and join them. She'd been shocked when her friends had shown up, demanded she pull her butt out of bed, shower and get dressed. Apparently, they wanted to cheer her up. This was certainly the way to do it. Especially since it was her birthday. The only problem was she hated her birthday and wished they wouldn't have bothered. They'd only just celebrated Peren's birthday and now it was Melanie's turn.

Less than two weeks ago she was living life to its fullest--partying, getting ready to head into her last year at the university and screwing a hell of a hunk. In the blink of an eye, it had all changed. She'd found herself in a whirlwind. Not fully understanding all that was going on around her but gathering enough information to know something was off. Seriously off. Random thoughts that didn't feel as though they were her own had begun to plague her waking hours.

The thoughts made little to no sense to her. Carrying an armful of books while wearing bobby socks and a poodle skirt was hardly something she was prone to do. Neither was obsessing over a man who had barely spoken five words to her. Yet, Green was all she could seem to concentrate on. She knew he was part of some secret operative team of men that worked for the government and that his specialty was science but that was it. Well, that and she knew she *had* to be around him. It was a compulsion she couldn't resist. Didn't even want to resist.

She glanced out at the dance floor and smiled as her gaze fell over her best friends, Missy and Peren. Each had their significant other with them, moving to the slow song. She'd known the women all her life and couldn't ever remember seeing them so happy. Their boyfriends Roi and Lukian had come roaring onto the scene a little over two weeks earlier. They had actually kidnapped, for lack of a better word, Melanie and her friends. Their intentions were honorable so she let it slip by. They were trying to protect Peren from an assassination attempt. They succeeded.

The only real complaint she had about the ordeal was how easily she'd given into one of the men--Lance. He'd been so charming and sexy that she couldn't seem to resist his pull. Melanie was anything but a delicate flower in the male department and wasn't ashamed to admit it. Though, her fun and fancy-free approach to men had caught up with her with Lance. But that wasn't something she wanted to focus on at the moment, regardless how much losing him pained her.

No. Right now, Melanie wanted to enjoy seeing her friends happy. She didn't want to dwell on how sick she'd been. How she hadn't been able to hold down anything of substance in over a week or how sleeping was a thing of the past. Now all she did was toss and turn, every joint on her body aching as her muscles tightened painfully.

Flexing her fingers, Melanie did her best to try to keep the cramps away but knew she would fail. She let her power up, careful not to let anyone around know what she was doing. The last thing she wanted was anyone to know who or what she was. It wasn't like her best friends would understand. No. They'd probably freak if they found out that she was anything but human.

They didn't even want to believe her when she'd try to tell them the truth--that Lance had shifted into an animal while they'd been having sex. There was no way they'd believe and understand that Melanie was more than what met the eye: a mythological creature, a Fae.

The feeling of being watched came over her and Melanie pulled her gifts back into herself quickly. Turning, she searched the club but found nothing out of the ordinary. Still, the feeling returned.

"Want to dance?" Wilson, one of the men who hung around with Roi and Lukian, appeared next to her with a silly grin on his face.

He was handsome, hell, they all were. How they managed to be a covert paramilitary anything was beyond her. The five of them looked like a sex squad, lethal, drop-dead gorgeous and mysterious. Melanie glanced over Wilson's shoulder and spotted Jon, a sandy blond with the most off-putting amber eyes she'd ever seen. He was talking with someone Melanie couldn't see.

Where's Green?

Wilson waved a hand before her face and grinned. "I should be offended that you seem to be interested in everything but me, but I'm not. Want to dance or spend the evening checking out Jon?"

Letting out a soft laugh, Melanie put her hand in his. It wasn't Jon she wanted to spend the evening checking out. The one she wanted hadn't come in with them and she hadn't wanted to be obvious and ask about him. It wasn't like her to pine after any man, especially not one who didn't seem interested in her in the least. In addition to that, Green, the man who had caught her fancy, was completely opposite the men she was normally attracted to. That being said, he was all she could think about.

As Wilson led her out to the dance floor she felt the intense weight of someone's stare on her once more and shivered. Wilson, who stood only one inch taller than her since she was in spiked heels, touched her bare shoulder. "You're cold."

"I'll be fine," she said, still unable to shake the feeling someone was watching them closely.

Wilson began to dance, matching her step for step. His brows rose. "Hey, you're good at this."

Smiling, Melanie nodded. "So are you. Care to tell me how you learned?"

He mumbled something under his breath and kept pace with her. Not really leading but keeping up just fine.

"I'm sorry, what was that?"

"Green taught me," he said, sounding as though it were a national secret he didn't want let out. Maybe it was.

The mere mention of Green made her body tighten. "Where is he tonight?"

"Who's Green?" Wilson gave her a mischievous smile as he lifted her hand in the air and spun her in a circle as *I've Got You Under My Skin* played in the background. The house band was amazing and a favorite of hers. She'd logged many hours staying past closing jamming with them. "He's here. He came with Jon."

He's here?

Immediately, her gaze went in Jon's direction with the hopes of seeing Green. The second her gaze fell upon the six-foot four-inch, muscle-bound man, dressed in a black suit with a charcoal gray shirt and black tie, her heart leapt to her throat. Green's close cut red hair was so dark it bordered on brown. His emerald eyes locked on her. She stopped dancing and simply stared at him.

"Thaddy," she whispered, unsure where or why the name had come out at all. It just felt right.

"Huh?" Wilson asked, placing his hand on her waist and moving in close to her. "Mel?"

"What?" She focused on Wilson and picked up where she'd left off with the dance. She'd spent her life dancing and singing. Her father said she came by it honestly, that it was something the women in his family did. Though he often joked she was the first woman who didn't step on others' toes while doing it.

"You just said 'Thaddy.' Who is that?"

"Hmm." She twisted and tapped the ball of her foot on the dance floor. "I'm not sure why I said it."

"Oh, hey, if you want in on the bet going about Green's first name you're welcome but I have to say, he doesn't strike me as a 'Thaddy.'"

Melanie drew back slightly. "You don't know your team member's first name?"

"Nope. Lukian knows it but the rest of us don't. I tried to bribe Lukian once. All I got out of him was a black eye so I stopped barking up that tree." He spun her in a circle before cradling her to his chest and moving to the beat.

"Not knowing his first name doesn't strike you as odd?"

Wilson's dark eyes raked over her slowly. "Baby cakes, everything in our lives is odd. You get used to it."

Baby cakes?

He leaned in closer. His warm breath skated over her lips. "Be honest with me. Do you really want to be here when you could be back at my place having your world rocked?"

Having my world rocked?

Not one to shy away from a lame come on, Melanie smiled. "Just because I fell into bed with your friend doesn't mean I hand it out to just anyone, Wilson."

"Really? You knew Lance all of an hour before he had you bent over with his dick crammed so far into you that you couldn't see straight."

Images of standing in the cemetery as they lowered a casket containing Lance's body into the ground hit her. She'd spent one night with him. It was purely sexual but that didn't lessen the pain of knowing he'd been senselessly ripped from this world and hearing someone who claimed to be Lance's friend speak so callously of him seriously pissed her off. It didn't bother her that Wilson was insinuating she was a whore. Melanie was pissed over Wilson's disrespect of his fallen brother. "Do you treat all your friends like this? Do you talk about them with nothing short of disgust in your voice when they only just passed away?"

"No," he said, his jaw line tightening. "I only talk about blonde bimbos who show up out of the blue, fuck my friends and leave their head so screwed up they end up getting themselves killed. And you can get the idea of sinking your claws into Green out of your empty head. I don't really give a damn about what will happen to you," he raked his gaze over her, "what *is* happening to you. I won't let you pull a black widow on him, too."

What the hell is he talking about? Pull a black widow?

Melanie glared at him. "I'm a bimbo, huh? Tell me, is that because I fucked Lance and not you, or do you just have that opinion about all women--blonde ones in particular?"

Wilson drew her in more, tightening his hold on her waist. "I've got nothing but respect for Peren and Missy. They were fated to be part of us, of our group. You weren't. And it disgusts me how everyone is all too willing to force a man who has no interest in you to commit the rest of his life to you because you couldn't keep your legs shut."

"What are you talking about?" she asked, completely lost. Wilson had seemed like a nice guy but here he was treating her like an ignorant slut. It wasn't the first time in her life a man had treated her in such a manner and it wouldn't be the last.

"I'm talking about you spreading those long legs of yours and entrapping two men at one time." A wicked grin spread over his face. "Want to give me a go? I'm interested to see if your pussy is worth dying for. Green is a fucking, bleeding heart. He'll fall for the 'poor helpless me' act and spend the rest of his life groveling at your feet. He can't help it. He's weak like that."

Enraged, Melanie drew her fist back fast and slammed it into his cheek, not bothering to hide her own supernatural strength. How dare he talk about Green that way?

Wilson staggered and she followed quickly, her hand throbbing and her breathing ragged. "You will not talk about him like that. He is not a weak, bleeding heart, Wilson. Green is a complicated man who doesn't wear his emotions on his sleeve, act like a jackass or feel the need to prove how much of a man he is by beating the living shit out of things. Because he's not outwardly violent means nothing!"

She shoved him hard and could have sworn the corners of his mouth curved upwards. *Did he think this was funny?*

"You can call me whatever the hell you want to. You can accuse me of being a bimbo blonde whatever, but you will *not* talk about a man who would do anything for someone he calls a friend. Understand me?"

Wilson shrugged. "Like I give a shit if Mr. Science Geek thinks of me as a friend or not."

Melanie gritted her teeth. She wanted to use her power to zap Wilson's ass to next week but she held back. Barely. "Never let me hear you making fun of Green for being a genius again. That man's mind never stops racing with ideas, theories and things you couldn't dream of understanding." She pointed at him as if it would help make it all clear. "Imagine what that must be like--living in a world where every time you speak, you know someone is going to make fun of you for what comes out of your mouth, that someone who doesn't understand will belittle you to make themselves feel better."

He put his hands up in a surrender position but Melanie didn't let up. Hearing Wilson say those things about Green made something in her snap. She knew she was being irrational. Hell, she didn't even really know Green. Sure, she'd been around him several times over the course of the last two and half weeks but they'd never really had a complete conversation. She wasn't even sure where she was coming up with her information about him or why she felt as passionate as she did about him. She only knew that she did.

"Wow, here I thought you were a pair of legs and an easy fuck. I'd have never guessed that under the obvious man-eater exterior you had a heart. Next you'll be trying to convince me you have a brain, too."

Melanie went to hit Wilson again but found herself being lifted off the ground by a pair of large arms. Heat rushed through her as the person holding her set her down and slid their hands over her torso slowly.

Turning, she found Green staring down at her with nothing short of rage on his face. She drew back. "I didn't mean to upset you. I just...."

He cupped her cheek and ran his thumb over her lower lip. His expression softened instantly. "Would you excuse me a moment?"

She nodded, too stunned to say a word.

Green turned and tipped his head back and forth, looking scary as hell. She watched as he struck out fast, knocking Wilson on his ass. Everyone stopped dancing and from the way Lukian and Roi froze with equally wide-eyed looks on their faces, they were as shocked as she was that Green leveled Wilson.

Roi smiled wide. "Damn, I bet that felt good. My turn." He made a move toward Wilson and Missy planted her five-foot, three-inch self in his path. Roi, equally as tall as Green, came to a grinding halt, instantly looking like a whipped puppy. "Fine but I still think it would feel great to slug Wilson."

Lukian arched a brow and pushed his chin-length, wavy, black hair back from his face. "Do I even want to know why you hit him?"

"No. You should just be happy I didn't kill him," Green said, his voice deep and his posture rigid. He stared down at Wilson. It wasn't a side of Green she expected to see. Hell, Melanie didn't expect to get to see any part of the man, let alone his violent side. "Set foot near her again, even glance at her, and I will kill you. Am I making myself clear enough for you? I'd hate to speak over your head, though, it is *so* very easy to do. And you should probably know that along with my affinity for science and the human body comes the knowledge of torture techniques you can't possibly fathom."

Roi formed an "O" with his mouth and shot Lukian an odd glance. "Never thought I'd hear myself say this but do you want me to restrain Green, Captain?"

Lukian's gaze fell upon Melanie. She didn't want to hear his answer. No part of her wanted Green to be dragged out by anyone. Moving forward quickly, she took hold of Green's muscular arm and tugged. "Thaddy, Thad, don't ... err ... I mean, Green. Don't. He's not worth it."

Green stilled and Lukian gasped. Melanie replayed what she'd just said through her head and sighed. "I'm so sorry, Green. I don't know why I called you Thad. Just please stop."

"He owes you an apology, Elizabeth."

Lukian gasped again. Apparently, it was habit forming.

Melanie snorted. "I'll take satisfaction out of punching him. I don't need his--hey," she looked over at Missy, "way to tell everyone my middle name. Gee, can I get a Melanie Elizabeth Daly out of someone so I feel like my father is yelling at me and I'm three-years old again?"

Missy shook her head, waves of black hair fell over her tiny shoulders. "Mel, I didn't tell him your middle name."

She didn't stop to think too hard on what Missy had said. Instead, Melanie pulled on Green's arm. "Please, Thad, don't."

Wilson got to his feet just in time for Jon to come rushing in. "Uhh, people. I don't know or care what's going on here but we're drawing a crowd. And I think we can agree that's a bad thing."

Peren slid around and stood before Lukian. She glanced at Melanie. "Sweetie, why do you keep calling Green, 'Thad' and varying forms of it?"

"Because it's my name," Green said softly, still refusing to back down or look at her.

A collective gasp went through the men.

Yep, habit forming.

Jon shook his head. "No fair telling her your name and making us spend years guessing. That's cheating. No way is she winning the pot."

Chapter Three

Green stood still as he tried to soak in what was happening around him. Last night he'd been blowing up buildings and tonight he wanted to blow up his own teammate. How he'd held back from ripping Wilson's head clean off his shoulders was a mystery to him. The rage tearing through him was a foreign feeling. One he wasn't sure he liked, but knew he was powerless to stop.

There had been something about Melanie that had caught and held his attention from the moment he met her but he never expected it to be what he thought it might be. There was no way Melanie was his Elizabeth--his wife who had passed away some fifty years ago while trying to give birth to his child. In the end, Green was left burying two people he loved, his family.

Hearing Melanie call him "Thaddy," the nickname Elizabeth had used for him when she was in a playful mood shook him to the core. The minute he'd screwed up and called Melanie by Elizabeth's name only to find it was hers as well, he'd fought the urge to throw her over his shoulder and run with her as fast as he could.

The very idea that Wilson had insulted her the way he had still had Green wanting to invent a new form of execution. He glared at him.

Wilson straightened his suit and winked. "I thought you might have some aggression in there somewhere, Green. Sorry I had to go about getting it out the way I did."

Huh?

Wilson nodded towards Melanie. "I'm sorry about what I said, Mel. I was just sick of waiting for the genius here to get around to coming to you. Are we cool? I didn't mean any of it. I swear. I've got nothing but respect for you. Honest. You can hit me a few more times if it'll make you feel better. I deserve it but I promise that I only wanted to provoke the big guy here."

Green shook his head. "You were nasty to her to get me to intervene?"

"Hey," Wilson's smirk was cocky enough to make Green want to hit him again, "I was all out of ideas. It's clear you two are interested in one another. I thought playing off what a gentleman you are might work. It did. Happy?"

Roi burst out laughing and Missy elbowed him hard. "Ouch. Sorry, but you have to admit it was a good idea. Plus, I can't ever remember a time in my life that Green threw the first punch or threatened to use his brains to come up with freaky torture techniques, hell, any torture techniques."

Melanie tugged on Green again and he couldn't deny her any longer. Turning, he locked gazes with her. She smiled wide and winked. "Come on."

Green didn't look back at the others. He just followed Melanie, lacing his fingers with her long delicate ones. The woman drove him mad with need. His cock seemed to be in a permanent state of ready around her and walking proved to be an issue. Thoughts of sinking into her, burying himself so deep that they'd lose track of where he stopped and she began besieged him.

Snap out of it.

It had been fifty years since he'd had sex with anything more than his hand. As an I-Op, a genetically-altered superhuman, his sperm could kill a human. If she survived the first night and he got her pregnant, she would die before the child was born. Carrying a supernatural child was too taxing on a human female. He'd learned that lesson first hand with his own wife.

He'd met her, fallen in love and asked her hand in marriage. Elizabeth had accepted. They'd married and she'd become pregnant the night of their wedding. Eight and a half months later, she fought for her life and that of their child's on a table before him. It was a battle she wasn't strong enough to win and one he couldn't fight for her.

Lukian had been with him when it happened. It was Lukian who had to pull him away from Elizabeth's side as he stood there begging her to come back to him, all the while knowing she was already long gone. Until that point, none of the I-Ops knew their sperm could be fatal to a human female.

Missy and Peren both carried an ample amount of supernatural DNA. In truth, they carried more strands of it than any of the I-Ops did. Lukian was a full-blooded lycan and had been born that way. Roi carried Lukian's wolf DNA in him and was in essence Lukian's brother because of it. Wilson carried the DNA of a rat due to another lab's screw up and Jon carried the DNA of a tiger. Their newest member of the team, Eadan, was a full-blooded Fae and Melanie's brother.

Green wasn't like the rest of the team. No. He hadn't been injected with a strand of animal DNA, nor had he been born that way. He'd been in his early thirties and working for the government on a project intent on creating a superhuman. A full-blooded were-panther had been captured and caged. Green was never told that it wasn't a normal panther, nor was he one of the scientists that experimented on it. When it broke free it attacked and slaughtered almost all of the scientists in the lab, but for some reason it hadn't killed him. Instead, it left him alive but infected with its DNA.

It had taken Green years and years to learn to control the beast of the panther that now resided in him. He'd never once given any thought that his condition could be deadly to anyone else or transmitted through his semen. That's why the I-Ops were freakish about wearing condoms when they were having sex even though they themselves couldn't catch or carry human diseases. And it was part of the reason why Melanie now suffered and was dying but didn't know it. In theory she could carry one of their children, if she had enough Fae blood in her but the separation from Lance wouldn't permit it.

She'd given herself to Lance, an I-Op who had been created from Green's very own strand DNA, making him a brother by blood. The condom had broken when Lance had lost control of his beast, shifting partially in her when he came. That meant he filled her with semen loaded with were-DNA. It also meant he had begun the claiming process. If he'd have bitten her, she would have been considered his wife. The possibility she was also with Lance's child was great. The thought of her being with Lance did hurt, but the idea that a tiny piece of his brother, by way of DNA, might live on in some fashion eased that.

When Lance died, his connection with Melanie didn't. The withdrawal she suffered from now was fatal unless someone with matching DNA stepped in and claimed her for his own. Green was the only other person with Lance's

DNA. It was his responsibility to care for her now. By all standards, he should have been livid at having a woman that he had no choice but claim dropped in his lap. That wasn't the case at all.

From the moment he'd laid eyes on Melanie he'd dreamt of sliding in and out of her perfect body, seeing her vivid blue eyes stare up at him while she accepted all that he had to offer her. It took everything in him not to reach out and run his fingers through her long blonde locks.

The silver dress she wore dipped down so low in the back that it just barely covered her ass and the slits on the sides of it left her long legs teasing him. When she turned to face him, her low-cut V-neck dress left the majority of her breasts showing. She didn't have a modest bone in her body. The Fae in her blood probably had something to do with that.

A low growl emanated from deep within him as he moved his body in front of hers, not wanting every other man there to see what was his. Melanie laughed and brought their joined hands to her cheek. She was soft and smelled delicious.

"Thank you for what you did, though I wish you wouldn't have."

"Why?"

She smiled. "Because peaceful men shouldn't feel as though they have to resort to violence."

He glanced around her and laughed softly. "Where's the Melanie I met two weeks ago?"

"Oh, the one who would say or do whatever or whoever was on her mind?"

The idea of her being with anyone but him set his nerves on edge. Green did his best not to let it show. She was entering her mid-twenties, was beautiful and carried old faerie blood in her. Like it or not, she was a sexual diva by nature. It was something he'd have to learn to control or live with. If she was half as strong willed as he suspected her to be, then he'd have a lifetime worth of men coming on to her. "Yes. That one."

She held tight to his hand and stared down at it. "I don't know. She's here somewhere."

He nodded and noticed her favoring her neck, stretching it as though she were in pain. Knowing she probably was made his chest tight. "You okay? Peren mentioned you've been a little under the weather."

It was the understatement of a lifetime.

Melanie nodded, as she ran her thumbs over his hand. "Don't laugh, but I feel better around you."

That made sense. Her withdrawal from Lance would lessen by just being close to Green. In theory, he could spend forever just being near her and keep her safe, but that wasn't enough for him. He wanted her for himself but after suffering a devastating loss he wasn't sure he was ready to open his heart again--especially not to a woman who made seducing men an art form.

Reaching up, she loosened his tie and began to lift it over his head. As Melanie rose to her tiptoes her mouth moved dangerously close to his. Green fought the primal urges she was causing to rip through his body and tipped his head down for her to get his tie completely off. The action left his lips brushing hers. A spark flared between them and he knew if he dared to give in, he'd take her and fuck her against the wall in front of everyone. That wasn't something he wanted to do so he held back.

She eased his tie off, reached into his jacket and stuffed it into his pocket before she began to unbutton his shirt. Green couldn't help but smile. Melanie was so very different from any other woman he'd ever met--including Elizabeth. It was most likely the old faerie blood Melanie carried in her that allowed her to pick up on details of his life. She couldn't be his Elizabeth. Could she? No, that was impossible.

She's sensitive. Psychic abilities run rampant in the Fae.

"Are you trying to undress me in public?" he asked, with a hopeful look. The idea had occurred to him. He glanced at one of the curved sofas lining the back wall and smiled. Thoughts of laying Melanie on her back, undressing her and licking every inch of her body filled his mind.

"Would undressing you be a bad thing?"

Some Enchanted Evening came on and a stab of guilt went through Green. It had been one of the songs that played at his wedding reception. Suddenly, his desire to spend the rest of his life with Melanie seemed so selfish, so wrong.

She didn't seem to notice his mood shift. That or she didn't care. No. Melanie continued her slow striptease of him, taking his jacket off him and laying it on the back of an empty chair. Without a word, she returned, cuffed each of his sleeves and pressed her body to his. "Mmm, that's much better. Now, dance with me."

"Melanie, I…"

She hooked her finger in his belt loop, pulling him to her, making his heart pound with a fury he thought for sure would cause it to burst. Melanie put her hands in his and winked. "I'm not allowed to start until you do. You value your toes too much."

Green gasped and did his best to not squeeze her hands too tight. She'd somehow managed to repeat what Elizabeth used to say almost verbatim. As Melanie kicked her right foot out and rolled her body towards him she left him panting on the inside. The swirling feeling in his mind was already leaving him fogged at best, having Melanie's lush, tempting body moving in close to his only added to it.

As he drew in her sweet scent, a cross between lavender and lilac, he couldn't stop himself from bending down and pulling Melanie into his arms, swaying slowly and listening to the steady beat of her heart. He moved with her, dancing across the open and extravagant lobby.

She was an amazing dancer and Green found himself smiling as he spun Melanie down the length of his arm. She tapped one foot out and then did it again. She did another step-heel and Green's chest tightened.

"You know how to tap dance?" he asked, staring at her with nothing short of rapture on his face.

"Yes. Are you going to make fun of me?" She sounded so vulnerable, so different than he thought she'd be. "I spent my childhood learning all types of dance. I drove my father nuts with it but he was good about indulging me."

"Why would I make fun of you?"

He pulled her back into him and rocked back and forth with her. She licked her lower lip and sent need slamming through him. "Wilson told me that you taught him to dance. Is that true?"

Green couldn't hide the smile on his face. "Why? Are you going to make fun of me? Let me tell you, it was a chore. I thought the boy was born with two left feet. Turns out, he just needed to be taught his left from his right."

The large smile she flashed him left him moving even closer to her, as if it were even possible. As the song drew to an end, Green found himself wishing it would go on forever. "How about I take you in there and do this for real?"

A man came walking out from the restaurant portion and Green recognized him as the manager. The man spotted Melanie and his eyes lit up. He was pushing forty and was too old for her.

Ha. I'm way *too old for her then.*

"Melanie, come and treat us to something special," he said, glancing at Green. "Bring your boyfriend."

He waited for Melanie to correct the man as to his status to her. When she laced her fingers through his, he had to fight the urge to kiss her.

"Oleg, I don't want to embarrass myself anymore than I have in front of Thad but thank you."

Green stared down at her, still unsure how it was she knew his name but loving the sound of it falling from her lips too much to care.

Oleg put his hand up. "Oh, sweetie, in case I miss you later, happy birthday."

Birthday?

Melanie smiled. "Thank you."

"You haven't been in for close to three weeks. We miss hearing you sing as we close up and you look like you've lost weight," Oleg said, narrowing his gaze on Melanie. "You're skinny enough to start with. Are you feeling okay?"

"I'm fine. Really."

Oleg nodded and headed off in the other direction. Melanie rubbed her neck again, clearly in pain. Green slid behind her, put his hand on her slender shoulders and began to rub them.

Sighing, she melted back into his body, causing his cock to throb madly. Part of him wanted to back away to avoid ejaculating but the other half of him refused to lose contact with her. His mouth burned for the change, to be allowed to shift into panther form and claim her as his own-- something he'd never done before.

The song changed. Melanie grabbed his hand and turned her face a bit. "Promise you'll play this for me again on the piano sometime. Please?"

He stilled and listened closer to the song. It was one of many he used to play on the piano for Elizabeth while she sat next to him on the bench, her belly swollen with his child and her eyes wide with excitement. The memory was bittersweet. While he'd loved having her there with him, being reminded she was gone stung. Melanie needed to curb her senses and stop reading him or he'd be an emotional mess in no time flat. "Melanie, stop."

"Stop what?"

"You know what. No more. I mean it."

She let go of his hand instantly. "Sorry, umm, I don't know why I asked you to play the piano." As she went to walk away, the compulsion to pull her back to him was great. He gave into it.

It was Melanie who refused to allow anything further to take place. She cast a nervous glance at him. "This is where I cut out. Thanks for the dance, Thad ... err ... Green."

He could almost feel her confusion over his behavior. He wanted to draw her back into his arms and show her how sorry he was. It was her birthday, she was in pain and he was being moody with her for simply requesting he play a song. Granted, she was somehow tapping into painful memories from his past but still, she didn't deserve to be treated badly.

Hearing Wilson say those ugly things to her had set Green off in a rage like no other. It was odd to hear Melanie defend him like she truly knew him. She forced a smile to her face as she headed towards the front door.

"Melanie?"

"I need some fresh air," she said, softly. "Go head back in with your friends. It was nice to finally talk to you. Night, Green."

Dismissed, but not deterred, Green shook his head. "I'd rather not go back in without you."

"Goodnight, Green."

"Wait, are you leaving?" he asked, doing everything he could not to pull her to him and hold her tight.

"I'm tired and my head is killing me. Would you tell everyone I said thanks?" She shivered slightly as she headed for the door. The dress she wore teased Green with "almost" glances at her lush ass.

He swallowed hard and grabbed his suit jacket from the back of the chair. "Melanie, here, put this on."

She glanced back at him and then the jacket. Her blue eyes widened and she arched a brow. "No. Thank you though."

He looked down at his jacket, unsure why she stared at it like it was deadly. "You're cold. It's a jacket. Its job is to warm someone. Let it perform its function."

She locked gazes with him. "I don't want the jacket and I don't want your sympathy. Wilson may have been trying to upset you but what he said was true. I'm just some whore who dropped into your lives and your heart is so big you'll do anything to help someone in need. I enjoyed the dance and your company--well, the part where you weren't feeling guilty over being near me."

He gasped. *She'd picked up on his feelings?*

"Melanie, I think you--"

"Goodnight, Doc Smart."

He froze. "Doc Smart" was what Elizabeth called him the first day they'd met. He clenched his fists. "I'd appreciate it if you'd stop reading me. I think you know what I mean."

Her brow furrowed. "Huh?"

"You keep bringing up things you shouldn't know about. I'd rather you didn't."

Melanie snorted. "What? You think I'm like a fortune teller or something? Umm, sorry to disappoint there, Green, but I'm not." She rolled her eyes. "You're the last person I want to fight with right now." Her eyes glistened with moisture. "Just once, I'd like to part ways without one of us angry or ending up in tears." With that, she turned and left.

Chapter Four

Green stood there, watching her leave, knowing he should go after her but rooted in place. Peren walked out from the dining area, followed closely by Missy and glanced around. "Hey, have you seen Melanie?"

"Umm, she wanted me to thank you both for tonight."

Missy's eyes widened. "What? She left?"

He nodded.

Peren covered her mouth. "Oh, gawd, we didn't get out her cake yet or anything. We didn't even say 'happy birthday.' She probably thinks we forgot again like we've done every other year."

Missy shook her head. "Don't kick yourself too hard. I was married to her brother and he forgot all the time, too. In fact, I'm betting Eadan hasn't even wished her a happy one yet, either. Melanie never makes a big deal about it. She celebrates everyone else's with flare but doesn't bring hers up at all. It's almost like she's ashamed she's having one. It's weird."

"She's getting worse," Peren said, tears coming to her eyes. "I can feel her fading more and more each day. At this rate...." She choked up.

Missy glanced at him. "No. Shh, she'll be fine. Won't she, Green?"

Peren wiped her cheeks. "Wait a minute, how is Melanie getting home? She rode with Lukian and me." Her eyes widened.

The second Missy grabbed Peren's arm, Green knew Melanie was walking. He clutched his jacket and headed towards the door. "I'll get her."

"No," Peren said, taking him by surprise. "We'll get her. She's *our* friend. *We* love her and actually care what happens to her."

Missy arched a brow. "Peren?"

Green stared down at the five-foot six-inch, auburn haired woman. "I care about what happens to her."

Peren snorted. "Lukian told me why it was he was shocked to hear her call you by your name and why you said the name Elizabeth." She glared at him. "Melanie isn't a charity case and she's not what everyone assumes she is--an air-head blonde. She's smart, Green. Very smart and has a heart of gold even though she doesn't see it. She is an amazing young woman whose life is being cut short because of your 'brother' and his inability to control his shifting. She was practicing safe sex. It's hardly her fault he changed partially into a panther. He terrified her, and Missy and I lied to her face about it--telling her it was her imagination. She's going to die because of me. Had she not been trying to give me a nice birthday night out, she wouldn't have been with us."

Green went to speak but Peren tossed her hand up and cut him off. "She would have been at college, not being pushed into the back of a van full of strangers. She wouldn't have met Lance and she would be safe right now--not dying a painful death. Do you know that I've spent almost every night with her and she cries in her sleep?" Peren blinked back tears. "She can't eat and the little bit of rest she gets is fitful."

"I can help her," Green said, fisting the jacket.

Peren shook her head. "No, you can't. My husband doesn't need to tell me what he's thinking. I can feel it and the minute he heard the name Elizabeth fall from your lips his thoughts were that you couldn't do this--that emotionally it would tear you apart and leave Melanie devastated *if* she managed to survive, mated to you, only to find out you aren't capable of letting go of the past. I refuse to see her live a life where she is second best in her husband's eyes. *We'll* get her home and take care of her. You can do us all a favor and keep your distance. *We'll* handle talking her into going to South America. We don't want your help!"

Her words where harsh and they hurt. Mostly because they were true.

"Let's go tell Lukian and Roi we're leaving," Peren said, guiding Missy back into the main part of the restaurant.

Green headed toward the door all the same and stilled when he spotted Melanie talking in the parking lot with Oleg. She was shaking her head but Oleg didn't seem to be listening. He lifted his arms out and Melanie smiled. She took his hand and he led her back towards the front entrance.

Taking a step back, Green watched her enter. Her gaze met his briefly before going to Oleg. "Go ahead. I promise to stand here and not move until the cab comes. You know, you're worse than my father."

He laughed. "Someone has to worry about you. Besides, your friends have a little something special they had us do for you to celebrate. Leaving before we bring it out would hurt their feelings."

Melanie sighed.

Oleg frowned. "Melanie, let them do this. They worked very hard not to forget this year."

"No, I'm just too weak to cast a memory spell on them so they can't do it this year," she said, barely above a whisper.

Green's supernatural hearing picked up on it instantly. She knew she had power? He hadn't sensed that in her before. He'd assumed she had no idea what she truly was.

Oleg headed off into the back and Melanie put her back to Green.

"Melanie?"

"Hmm?" she asked, not turning to face him.

"Do you think if I worked hard on pulling my foot out of my mouth you'd consider honoring me with another dance?"

Glancing over her shoulder, she winked at him. "You're not in the dog house, Thad. I'm just not feeling very well."

His heart beat faster as he stared at her. If he didn't know better, he'd have sworn it was Elizabeth standing there. But that was impossible.

Melanie's head jerked up and she took a step back from the doorway. Putting her hand out, she pushed him back as well. She stiffened and his built-in alarm went off. The smell of her fear only set him on edge more. "What's wrong, Melanie?"

"Nothing," she said in a hushed tone. It was a lie and he knew it. One of the gifts he'd developed over the years had been the sensing of truths. It was a gift normally reserved for vampires but he'd ended up with it all the same.

"Melanie?"

She sighed and glanced around nervously. Goose bumps formed on her arms and he knew she was scared. "Someone is watching us."

He glanced around, not sensing anything out of the norm. "Honey, you're beautiful. It's natural for men to want to watch you."

Had he really just told her that she was beautiful and used a pet name for her? She was drop-dead gorgeous, but the idea of spitting that out made him take a deep breath and wait on pins and needles for her response.

Melanie moved into his arms more. "Flattery will normally get you everywhere with me, but this is hard for me to explain. This is different. Someone," she put her palm against his chest, "is close. Closer than you'd want them to be."

Huh?

Green glanced over his shoulder, trying to sense something, anything that could help him understand what Melanie was going through. He got nothing. The way she clung to him told him she firmly believed whatever she sensed was real. That was enough to concern him.

A flash of auburn and a blur of black went past him. Green stiffened and jerked Melanie behind him a second before he realized the flash and blur were Peren and Missy. They stared around the large entrance way to the restaurant with equally cautious looks on their faces.

"Mel, you're back!" Missy said.

Lukian and Roi came rushing out as well. Lukian grabbed hold of his mate's arm lightly. "Peren, what in the hell is going on? Why did the two of you take off?"

Melanie poked out from behind Green. He tried to keep her behind him but she wasn't having any of that. "Peren? Missy?"

Peren locked gazes with her friend and sighed. "You're okay."

"Of course, she's okay," Green said, skimming his hand over Melanie's bare back and then desperately wishing he hadn't as his cock began to throb with need. "I'd never harm her."

Peren shook her head. "Green, I never in a million years thought you would. It's just that," she bit her lower lip and glanced at Missy, "we kind of ... umm ... is everything okay out here?"

Missy rolled her eyes. "Fuck this bullshit. Do you guys sense anything freaky going on or are we the only two getting a bad vibe?"

Roi snorted. "Trust my wife to cut to the chase."

"Your wife?" Melanie asked. She put her hand up fast. "Don't answer that. In fact, don't answer anything else. They're listening to us right now and the less they know about us the better. I can block the humans from sensing or seeing what's going on but I can't block whatever is listening from hearing us. It's hard for me to explain. Please don't ask me to right now. I'll answer questions later. Right now, I think we should go."

"Huh?" Missy asked, stealing the very word from Green's lips. "Melanie?"

Peren touched Missy's shoulder and locked gazes with Green. When she spoke, she directed it at Melanie but never looked away from him. "Melanie, why don't *we* take you home to get some rest? You haven't been acting like yourself lately."

* * * *

Ignoring Peren, Melanie tipped her head, listening to the tiniest of buzzes as it rode the air. Something seemed to press in on her, making it harder to breathe than it should. She gave in, doing her best to figure out what, if anything, her body was trying to tell her. A clear image of men, dressed all in black hit her. She saw them inching their way around, armed to the teeth, reeking of evil.

What are they hunting?

Closing her eyes, Melanie concentrated. She gasped. "The females."

"What?" Green asked, sliding his hand down her back.

Her gaze went to her best friends. Peren's brow furrowed. "Mel, hon?"

"I-I, umm, don't feel very well. I want you and Missy to get away from ... err ... I mean could you take me home?"

"Mel?" Missy asked, moving toward her slowly, as if she were afraid Melanie would bite. "What's going on? Do you want Green to drive you home?"

Peren gave Missy a hard look and Missy shrugged. "What? I happen to disagree with you, Peren. I think he can and will have a future with her."

Melanie's eyes widened. "No! I want you and Peren to come with me now! We have to go!"

Green was on her in an instant, wrapping his arms around her. "Melanie," the very sound of her name falling from his lips helped to calm her, "you can tell them anything and I do mean *anything*."

"What do you mean?" she asked, doing what she always did when she needed to hide who and what she was--she played dumb. It had worked wonders for her all her life. She played into what people's perception of her was--blonde bimbo.

He pulled her tighter into his arms and pressed his mouth to her ear. Her entire body lit as she wrapped her arms around him. "Melanie, don't hide from us--from me."

It was on the tip of her tongue to tell Green all her secrets. She held back. Whoever was listening didn't need to know her life history. "I'm sorry."

"For what?"

Hugging him tight, she readied herself to be something she didn't want to be to him--a bitch. Drawing back, she ran a hand through her hair, squared her shoulders and let her inner vixen persona out to play. "I'm tired. I don't feel well and I'm bored out of my mind. Can I just get some support from my best friends, please?"

"Bored?" Green asked, barely above a whisper.

"Yeah, you're not exactly the most outgoing guy, Green. I can't believe I gave up a night of drinking and partying at the bar for this place." The pain that flashed in his eyes hurt her. She clenched her fist in an attempt to concentrate on anything but the urge to run to him, beg his forgiveness and wrap her arms around her Thaddy.

My Thaddy?

"You just stood in front of an entire dance floor shouting about how misunderstood Green is. I'm not buying you think he's boring in the least." Missy said, covering the distance between them quickly. "And you friggin' love this place. Every third time you'd run away when we were in high school, we'd find you here. Try another one. I'm not buying it. Why are you pushing him away? Melanie, what's going on?"

"Nothing." She had to fight not to look at Green. "I just want to...." She gasped as she felt a surge of evil around them.

Missy drew in a sharp breath. "I feel Fae power around us."

"What?" Melanie asked, unable to believe her life-long friend had just referred to something as Fae. *How the hell did Missy know about Fae?*

Eadan.

It hit her then. Melanie's brother, Eadan and Missy had been roommates. In fact, Missy was only now in the process of moving in with Roi. Eadan had to have told her about the Fae. That was the only explanation Melanie could come up with.

"Are you doing it, Melanie?" Missy asked, never missing a beat. "Is that what you're trying to hide from Green by being so mean to him? That you can do what your brother can?"

Melanie shook her head as her gaze locked on Green. "No, it's not me. It's someone else. Someone powerful. We have to go now! I'm not at full strength. Whoever this is could level me with one--"

A bone-crushing amount of power slammed into Melanie, causing her to stagger. Missy and Peren went down, both clutching their heads. The pain increased, feeling as though someone were driving nails straight into their skulls.

Peren screamed and Missy followed close behind. The men converged on them, surrounding them in a protective manner.

"What the hell is happening?" Lukian yelled.

Green dropped down next to Melanie and cupped her face. She blinked up at him as pain continued to stab through her skull. "Melanie, honey, talk to me. What's wrong?"

She tried to focus on him but the stench of evil was so great and the pressure in her head so powerful that she felt it might burst. Her power raced around her immediate area, sensing similar magik in both Peren and Missy. She sensed something else in both of them as well--babies.

She gasped.

"Pregnant," she bit out, reaching for them.

Green sighed. "I know you are, honey. That isn't causing this. Tell me what's happening."

She shook her head and pointed at Missy. "Not me. Pregnant. They're coming for the females because they ... uhh ... know they're ... ouch ... pregnant."

Roi growled out and took hold of Missy. "They are not touching my wife or child!"

"Peren, baby, talk to me," Lukian said, wrapping his arm around her.

"Hurts," Peren said. "Head hurts."

Knowing that whatever was happening could and would leave permanent damage if it continued, Melanie did the only thing she could think of. She decided to kick her power into high gear. She looked at Green. "Kiss me or move so Wilson or Jon can do it! Now!"

"What? They are not touching you!"

Lukian shoved Wilson towards Melanie. "If Green doesn't do it right this second, shoot him in the leg and kiss her! She's got Fae in her. So does Peren. Sexual stimulation of any kind cranks that part up."

Wilson's brows rose. "You want me to screw Green's mate? I'd give my right nut for a night with Melanie but Green would kill me. Need I remind you the guy took out an RPG dude with one friggin' shot while Roi was driving like a bat out of hell in the opposite direction? Uhh, thanks, but no. I was a little too present when he reminded me of his massive intellect and his ability to invent new torture techniques."

"I will kill you if anything happens to *any* of them," Lukian said, glaring at Wilson.

Melanie glanced at Green. "Please."

"I can't," he said, moving back and closing his eyes. "Jon, you do it."

Jon gasped. "Captain?"

Seeing it was pointless, the men would just continue to bounce it back and forth, Melanie pushed to her feet and rushed into the other room. She grabbed hold of the first man she spotted and yanked him into the outer lobby area with the rest of the team. He wasn't bad looking but he wasn't a certified stud like the ones behind her. Still, he'd do.

The man stared down at her with a shocked look upon his face. He was familiar. She'd seen him before. "I know you, you're the girl who sings when the place closes," he said, his eyes wide. "Why are you looking at me like that?"

Melanie captured his lips with hers and thrust her tongue into his mouth. Her power surged as their tongues locked. His hands went to her sides and with the dress she'd chosen, her sides were bare. As much as she needed stimulation to take her power to another level, she didn't want sex from this man. She wanted it from the man who had refused her--Green.

Taking hold of the man's wrists, she used her supernatural strength to pin his hands above his head and she continued kissing him feverishly. Melanie knew the man was aroused. She didn't need the confirmation of his erection pressing against her lower stomach.

Green growled and she ignored him. He'd blown his chance. Vaguely, she heard him shouting something and then the sounds of Wilson and Jon talking about how they couldn't hold him back much longer.

Her power went to full force just as she sensed whatever the evil was increasing its force. Melanie let go of the man and he stayed pressed to the wall, looking stunned and stupid. Smiling, she winked. "Sleep."

His eyes closed and he slid down the wall slowly. Jon cleared his throat. "Damn happy she didn't kiss me. Green would have had an easy kill, considering I'd have been unconscious."

Racing towards Peren and Missy, Melanie glanced at Green as Jon and Wilson released him. She gave him a hard look. He glanced away. She dropped down in front of Peren, cupped her face and pressed her mouth to Peren's. She let her power out. It flowed into Peren.

Melanie crawled to Missy and did the same thing, thrusting power into her as well. Both women stopped holding their heads and stared at Melanie. She smiled. "Guys have been waiting for us to kiss like that forever."

They let out shaky laughs.

Roi grabbed Missy to him. "The baby?"

Melanie let her power run out and over both women. She nodded. "Their babies are fine."

Peren shook her head. "I'm not pregnant."

Melanie gave her a droll look. "Ya sure, cuz I'm sensing a baby boy in there?"

"A son?" Lukian grabbed Peren. "I thought your scent had changed but I didn't want to say anything until...." He looked up at Melanie. "Thank you."

Peren grabbed Lukian's arm. "Men. Lots of men are moving in around the outside of the building. I think Melanie could sense them, that's why I can now."

Missy nodded. "They're armed to the teeth and she's right, they're coming for us--the females." Covering her stomach with one hand, Missy shook her head. "They know we're expecting and want us alive. They want Melanie too for other reasons."

Melanie's power wavered for a second and the glamour she'd tossed around them so the humans wouldn't sense anything dropped momentarily.

"Like hell!" Roi shouted, drawing the attention of other patron to the lobby.

Wilson waved at all of them. "Sorry, he's a huge fan of the big band era. Get's him all excited. Plus, he's been drinking so he might start trying to sing Sinatra soon. Go on back to your fun. We'll get him out of here."

Tossing her power back up and around them, she masked them from the humans once more. Melanie's hand picked then to cramp up on her. She hissed as she cradled it to her chest.

Green made a move to come to her but her glare stopped him in his place. She flicked power at him, assuring he couldn't get any closer. "Don't even think of touching me now, asshole."

Wilson came towards her, not seeming to care that she looked as if she wanted to spit nails. "You're in pain."

"I'm fine. Peren and Missy need to leave here now." She went to take a step and staggered. Pain took hold of her just as Wilson caught her.

"Mel?"

Coughing, she winced as her insides hurt. The taste of blood filled her mouth and she touched her lips gingerly. When she pulled her hand back, it was red. Wilson drew in a sharp breath. "Oh shit, Mel. Captain, she's coughing up blood."

"Melanie?" Green made another move to come to her but she shook her head.

"I said ... I'm fine."

"Honey, no. You're hurt."

"Mel, let him look at you," Peren said, her voice laced with concern.

"It'll go away. It always does."

Something hissed and the lights flickered. Raw energy shot out and around them. Melanie knew without looking that the humans in the other room would be rendered immobile by it. The power was familiar somehow. It was evil.

"What the fuck is going on?" Roi asked, backing Missy up and staring around the large lobby.

Suddenly, men dressed in black and carrying enough guns to take out a small army appeared from the shadows. All their weapons were trained on the men in the group. Three of the men in full black garb stepped forward. One removed his mask and Melanie's breath caught. It was a face she'd seen in her nightmares growing up. A face that struck fear in her.

Green, Wilson, Roi, Jon and Lukian all went to attack. It was a blur. A shot went off and one of the bad guys dropped to the floor. Out of the corner of her eye, Melanie was sure she spotted Lukian snapping a man's neck. She gulped and felt the force of familiar, old Fae power charging up around them. In an instant, all of the good guys were ripped back by an unseen force, leaving Melanie, Missy and Peren standing between them and the bad guys. Wilson staggered and bumped into her. It was oddly comforting to know at least one of the men ended up close to her. Though, she would have preferred Green.

"What the fuck? I can barely move!" Roi asked, sounding strained and pissed.

"Same here!" Jon shouted.

"Here too," Wilson said. "Feels like I'm in quicksand."

Lukian snarled. "Fae magik."

"You fucking son-of-a...."

Melanie glanced back at Green, shocked by his outburst. He was able to move a foot or so but seemed locked in a tiny area. His gaze was tight on her and something akin to worry filled his eyes. His gaze shot to Wilson who was the closest good guy to Melanie. "Protect her."

Wilson nodded, skimming his hand over the back of Melanie's arm. Unable to bear the thought of Green hurting, she turned and stared up into the face that haunted her dreams for so long and shook her head, not wanting to believe her own eyes. "You're not real," she said, moving into Wilson's arms. The bizarre sound that came from Green told her that he wasn't pleased with her actions but she was too caught up with the man before her to care.

The man stared out from blue-gray eyes. His jet-black hair hung to his waist and his skin seemed to shimmer. He laughed. The sound sent chills through her. He stared down at her and smiled. He was sexy in a dark, mysterious way but she knew better than to fall for his charms. He was pure evil.

"Melanie, my, how you've grown since our last meeting." He licked his lower lip and adjusted his cock through his black pants. "Mmm, you certainly are *all* woman now, aren't you?"

"You know this guy?" Wilson asked.

Green growled again.

She could do little more than stare at the man whom she'd come to believe was nothing more than a figment of her imagination.

The man glanced around. "Hmm, Daddy isn't here to come rushing in and protect his baby girl, is he? And we've established," his hot gaze raked over her, "that you aren't a baby anymore. I believe I will be spending more time in your bedroom now."

"Like hell you will!" Green shouted.

The man with black hair ignored him, keeping his gaze trained on Melanie instead.

"Ferdian, grab her and be done. The objective is to retrieve the females, not toy with one and risk it all. Krauss will rip our hearts out if we blow this," the man to the right of the newest threat said.

Ferdian?

It couldn't be. He was a figment of her imagination. He wasn't real. He couldn't be.

Ferdian glared at the man next to him. "It is my power that holds them in place or do you forget who and what I am? I shall do as I please. Krauss is not my master. I answer to no one. If anything, he should fear me. He is but a lowly human. Melanie and I have quite a history. Don't we?"

"Guess we know which asshole to kill first then," Roi bit out.

"If he lays one hand on her, I'll rip it off and cram it down his throat," Green said, his voice deeper than normal.

She shook her head as she stared up at Ferdian. "You're not real. You're the result of an overactive imagination. A manifestation I used to help me cope with power I was too young to control. That's all you are. I'm hallucinating. That's it or I'm crazy. Either way. You aren't real."

"That's your father talking, Melanie. I'm sure Medrawd thought it best to tell you it was all just a bad dream." He laughed wickedly. "I have not seen you since you were but a child, darling. So tiny. So scared of the man who you thought came out from under your bed. Tell me, did *Thaddy* ever come to save you? I know Daddy did, but what of this imaginary friend of yours? The one you told me would bite me for scaring you?"

Green made a slight choking sound. Melanie echoed it, shocked by Ferdian's words.

Wilson grabbed her arm. "You talked about Thaddy ... uh ... you know who when you were little?"

She shook her head and did her best to ignore the pain that continued to move through her. "No. I don't think I did but since I didn't think the crazy guy standing before us was real we might not want to take my answer to heart."

Ferdian laughed again and put his hand out. A ball of white light appeared in it. It filled quickly with an image of a little girl with white-blonde hair and blue eyes huddled at the top of her bed, the covers pulled up close, just under her eyes. She clutched a baby doll with short red hair and blue clothes. Moonlight filtered through the window and a pink, ballerina night light sat on a white bedside table.

Ferdian pointed at the image. "There you are, Melanie. What are you there, four years old maybe? Do you remember what you were scared of?"

Melanie staggered and Wilson wrapped his arms around her waist. Digging deep, she tried to draw upon the sheer will to live to gain her strength.

"You were scared of me, Melanie. Terrified I would return and force you tell me where she is." He glared at her and memories of terror he'd instilled in her flooded back. "Tell me where Elizabeth is and I will spare your friends' lives."

Green and Lukian gasped.

Yep, most certainly habit forming.

"Ferdian!" the man closest to him said. "This is not part of the plan. We are to seize the women and impregnate the blonde before the day is out. If memory serves, you requested the honor of being the one to do just that. We are not to--"

The sounds of Green and the others struggling against the magik holding them filled the air. They couldn't break free but Melanie didn't have the heart to tell them.

Ferdian shot power out at the man who dared to question him and he burst into flames. Wilson pulled Melanie closer and put his lips to her ear. "I think you should keep your middle name to yourself."

She nodded as she stared up at Ferdian. "I don't know who you're talking about."

It was a blatant lie but she wasn't about to tell him what he wanted to know.

"Lies, lies, lies," he said, sending power at Wilson.

Melanie pushed Wilson out of the way. He didn't go far since Ferdian still had a magikal hold on him but he moved enough. She put her hand out, absorbing Ferdian's power. It strengthened her a bit, helping her steady herself. Her eyes widened. There was no doubt in her mind Ferdian was powerful. She also knew he could kill all men present with no more than a thought. She wouldn't let that happen.

"Very good, Melanie," he said, eyeing her as though he were mentally undressing her. The second she felt magik creeping up and under her dress, she squared her shoulders and glared at him.

"Stop it."

"Stop what?" he asked, shrugging. The look on his face said he knew exactly what she was talking about.

"Stop trying to get your rocks off by touching me without touching me." She glared at him, hoping to keep his attention on her and off the men. "Know that if you try to touch me with anything else, magik or not, you will regret it."

Ferdian appeared impressed with her. "Oh, you still have the stubborn streak in you that I liked so much. You should probably know when I take you home with me I will beat it out of you, before I plant my seed deep within you, but for the time being, your resistance amuses me. In fact, you intrigue me greatly, Melanie. Why is that?"

"Because you clearly have a degenerative brain disorder, resulting in the lack of manners, originality and non-creepiness."

Wilson laughed under his breath. Green sounded as if he was being muzzled. She could only guess who was doing what to him but whatever was happening, it was best he remained silent. He seemed to have a hidden temper that liked to hit things.

"Melanie," Peren said evenly. "Stop provoking him. He's not the only one on the edge."

Did she mean Green too?

Ferdian glanced at Peren. "Save your breath. Melanie has never been one to back down from me. I admire that, to a degree. See for yourself." He tapped the white ball of light that held an image of her in it as a child and smiled.

It began to play again, showing the younger version of herself crying softly as she stared at the darkened room. It then showed Ferdian stepping into the picture. He had a goatee then, and wore long robes, leaving him looking sinister and regal. The sword at his side was big enough to terrify an adult, let alone a child.

"Hey there, Melanie," he whispered.

Melanie watched herself as a child, watched how scared she had been of the man as he reached out to her younger self....

Little Melanie jerked back and pulled the covers over her head. "Go away! You're not 'posed to be here."

He chuckled. "I know. I told you I would leave you alone if you just tell me where she is. Whisper it in my ear and I'll let you and your dolly be." He reached for the doll and the younger version of herself slapped his hand away.

"Don't you touch Chandler! He's mine! You're bad and not 'posed to be here!"

"Tell me where Elizabeth is. I know you know--you smell of her power. If I was not positive you came from your mother's womb, I would assume you were Elizabeth's child. You carry her scent, her power. Tell me where she is, Melanie. She must visit often for you to smell of her. It's very important I find her. She's in danger and I can help her."

"No. You lie. You're bad and she doesn't want to see you." The tiny version of Melanie stood and smacked Ferdian across the face so fast the man never saw it coming. She glared at him. "Thaddy will come and he'll bite you for being mean to me! He'll eat you." She made kitty noises and scratched at him with her fingers.

"Thaddy?" Ferdian asked, his eyes narrow. "Is Elizabeth with this person now?"

Little Melanie giggled and shook her head no. "I bet Thaddy thinks you taste bad because you are bad. Black heart. Evil to core." She spun in a circle and began to sing softly. "Black heart. Black heart. Eat you up. Eat you up. Spit 'em out. Spit 'em...."

Ferdian backhanded her, sending her crashing into the wall. "Those were Elizabeth's parting words to me. Where is she?"

Little Melanie held her cheek and glared at the man, her expression suddenly looking beyond her years. "Somewhere you can never hurt her again."

"You *will* tell me child." He seized hold of her baby doll and made it burst into flames.

Her eyes widened a second before she leveled a rather off-putting look on him. "Fix him, now, Ferdian. You will not harm anything or anyone I love ever again." The words came from the younger version of Melanie but they were said with the precision of an adult.

The man tipped his head, looking puzzled. He snapped his fingers and a new doll appeared. This one had long blonde hair like her own and bright blue eyes. "Tell me where Elizabeth is and you may have this dolly. See, she is much prettier than your other. She looks like you. Do you like her?"

Little Melanie glared at him, her cheek red where he'd slapped her and her gaze hard. "Chandler is a boy baby doll and he is perfect with red hair and green eyes. Bring him back or I will never tell you what you want to know."

"So, you do know where Elizabeth hides." He snapped his fingers and the doll she called Chandler appeared on the bed. She made a move to grab him and Ferdian caught her around the waist.

She screamed and he covered her mouth with his hand. Melanie bit him hard enough to draw blood. He dropped her and she stood tall, her nightgown stained red.

"Why you little--"

Tossing a hand in the air, little Melanie released magik and pinned Ferdian in place. A slow smile moved over his face. "Child, I do believe I like you. That is rare for me. In fact, I've hated every other child I've ever had the displeasure of encountering."

The tiny version of herself snorted still seeming much older than her years. "Trust me, Ferdian, the children hate you, too. It's mutual." She glanced at the doorway and lifted her hand. "You should know that Medrawd still hates you."

"Medrawd? You mean, your father?"

She nodded, a knowing smile moving over her face. "He is now. He hates you still, Ferdian. Hates what you did to Elizabeth. Medrawd would love nothing more than to get his hands on you."

"How is it you know my name, child? And why are your words suddenly that of someone much older?"

She continued to smile. "Someone whispered them in my ear. Someone who hates you almost as much as you hate yourself." She let her power out, it slammed into the door, crashing it into a hundred pieces. "Daddy! Daddy! Daddy!"

Lights flickered on in the hallway and a large man with shoulder-length blond hair rushed into the frame. Her father took one look at Ferdian and lifted his hands. Power shot out and sent Ferdian spiraling out of the image. The white globe of light faded fast, taking the image with it.

Melanie coughed and more blood came up.

Ferdian took a step towards her. "See, you know who and where Elizabeth is, Melanie. I know she's the one who told you about me. The one who whispers to you. Tell me now." His brow furrowed. "Are you bleeding?"

He made anther move for her and Wilson, Jon, Roi, Lukian and Green made a motion to move. The men in black aimed at them even though they couldn't get far. Melanie put her hand up. "Don't shoot them. I'll tell you. Let them go."

"Tell me first and then I will."

Closing her eyes slightly, Melanie let her gut instincts guide her. She let out a soft laugh. "Listen, old buddy, old pal, I've got about a week left, if that. They don't think I know I'm dying. I do. If you think I give a shit if these people live or die then you're stupider than I thought you were when I was four. By the looks of your portable viewing screen there, my opinion of you was low even then." She grabbed Wilson's hand and pulled him closer to her. "Here, kill this one. No one likes him."

Wilson's eyes widened and the rest of the people she was with gasped.

Melanie leaned over and coughed slightly. "A kiss from the whore before dying?" She didn't wait for him to respond, she pressed her lips to his, thrusting her blood into his mouth. With her blood, came her defense to their silver bullets. She drew back and put her hand out to Ferdian. "Christ, you are slow. Give me the gun, I'll shoot him myself."

Ferdian's brows rose. "Give the lady a gun."

"Are you mad?" the man asked.

He laughed. "Melanie is harmless. The woman grew up dancing, singing, living in a land of make believe. If she hits him it will be amazing. Now, Elizabeth, she's one I wouldn't want to see armed. The woman is lethal when provoked. It's part of what I love about her. Her little friend here is nothing to be concerned with. Though, I will be sinking my cock into her later. I can hardly pass up a body and spirit like that now, can I? Give her your gun. Let her prove herself."

The man next to Ferdian handed her a weapon reluctantly.

Turning, Melanie looked at Wilson and winked a second before she fired at his chest. The rest of his team went to charge at her but found themselves at the end of so many guns and still stuck behind Ferdian's power. They had no choice but to stand still.

Ferdian laughed. "Wise choice gentlemen, those are silver bullets they have there."

Melanie coughed and more blood came up. "Cut the shit and let's go find Elizabeth. I'll even let you stare at my ass the entire way."

The man next to Ferdian went for Peren. Melanie shot him in arm. He lurched back and stared at her with wide eyes. She winked. "Did I say you could move?"

The man glared at her. "Lucky for you, your aim is shit or I would gut you now."

Melanie put her hand out and smiled, drawing upon her power. "Gun!"

The semi-automatic gun one of the men had flew at her. She caught it with one hand and aimed at the bad guys to her left. Without looking, she fired, careful to let off the trigger where she knew the I-Ops to be standing. She kept her gaze on the man next to Ferdian the entire time, watching the shock on his face and loving every second of it. When she was done, she smiled. "I trust you will find all of your men injured or dead and none of mine are. As you can see, my aim is not an issue. I was being kind by not shooting you in the head before. If you try to touch my friend again, I'll put one between your eyes, asshole."

Ferdian laughed from the gut. "Oh, I can see why Elizabeth likes you. You have her spirit. Her spunk." He glanced around the room. "Her aim. Though, you forgot about your man, the one you shot. He's dead."

Wilson laughed as he rolled to his feet slowly. "No. Actually, I'm not. I don't know how I'm not. But I'm not."

Melanie smiled. "It's the Fae blood. We aren't allergic to silver. I sensed you were. I'd apologize for shooting you but you did antagonize the 'science geek' earlier."

"Who, Gr--"

Melanie thrust magik out at Wilson, shutting him up before he could say anymore.

Chapter Five

Ferdian stared at her and clapped. "Very good, Melanie. Elizabeth has taught you well. Now, tell me where she is. She and I have much to discuss."

Laughing, Melanie shook her head. "She's dead. She's somewhere you can't ever hurt her again and she's not scared of you anymore."

"You lie."

"Nope. She gave her immortality up to keep you from being able to track her and died knowing she was loved. She died knowing you couldn't keep her soul--that it was free to live on. She died free from your clutches. Free from your black heart. Evil to the core."

"No!" Ferdian screamed, his power made the room shake. "You lie."

"Why would I lie about something like that?" she asked, unsure as to what she was even talking about. She was beyond lost but continued to go with what her gut told her to.

"My wife is not dead!"

"Your wife?" Green asked, speaking for the first time. The tiniest buzz of Fae power pushed away. It wasn't her power and it wasn't Ferdian's. Someone had been keeping Green silent with magik but whom? Peren cursed under her breath and Melanie couldn't help but wonder if her friend had something to do with Green's silence.

Ferdian ignored him, so did Melanie. She focused her attention on Ferdian. "Elizabeth never wanted to be yours. You wrongfully claimed her without her consent and forced her to live for years in fear of you, of your wrath, of what you would do to her friends, her family. But she figured out how to get away."

Melanie tipped her head a bit, amused by the emotional pain she knew she was causing Ferdian. "She knew if she gave up the one thing that kept her tied to you, her immortality, she would be free to live her life as she pleased, to love who she wanted."

Ferdian threw power at her and she caught it with one hand. Spinning it around, she laughed and threw it back at him. His eyes widened. "How? Only Elizabeth could do that. Only she was strong enough...." He shook his head. "You lie. Medrawd has her hidden somewhere. He would never let his baby sister give up her immortality. Never. He was like a father to her. He would never let...."

He stared at Melanie and a slow lecherous smile slid over his face. "Like a father to her?" He took a step towards her. "Tell me, Melanie, when was it Elizabeth died? Was it recent or was it before you were born?"

"Does it matter?" she asked, unsure where his line of questioning was going.

He nodded. "Very much. You drop the news that my wife is dead on me out of the blue, yet I get the feeling you have known about her passing for some time. Did you know when you were little, Melanie?"

Something made her turn and glance at Green. His emerald eyes locked on her and he looked as interested in her answer as Ferdian was.

In an instant, Ferdian was in front of her, cupping the back of her neck and pressing his body to hers.

"Get your hands off her," Green said with a dangerous edge to his voice.

Something moved behind her and she knew it was Green. How he'd managed to break Ferdian's hold was a mystery to her. Ferdian put his hand up and unleashed a wave of power that made all of the members of Green's team sound as if they were in pain.

Melanie grabbed Ferdian's hand in hers. "Stop it! Don't hurt him ... uh ... them!"

"Stop it, you're killing them!" Missy yelled.

Ferdian stared closely at Melanie. "You value their lives?"

She nodded. "Yes."

He closed his fist and the magik dropped. From the sound of the thuds around her, so did the men. "There, they will live. They will be sore but alive. Consider it my gift to you."

"For what?"

"For helping me find my wife."

Puzzled, Melanie's brow furrowed. "I haven't helped you find Elizabeth. I told you she was--"

He cupped her cheek. "Look at me."

She did.

Ferdian whispered something in ancient Fae and power sprinkled over her. He smiled down at her as a large mirror appeared out of no where.

Her inner alarm went off. Something told her to run. She listened to it. Ferdian seized hold of her just as she caught sight of Green struggling to get to his feet. She broke free of Ferdian's grasp and rushed to Green's side.

"Are you okay?" she asked, grabbing Green's muscular arm and doing her best to get him to his feet. She got him as far as his knees when Peren and Missy drew in sharp breaths.

"Mel, what's happening?" Missy asked.

Glancing up, she found Ferdian leaning against the oversized, gilded-edged mirror with a sinister smile upon his face. He picked at his fingernail as he quirked a brow. "Oh, Melanie, you *more* than helped me find Elizabeth."

She looked at the mirror and froze as she watched her reflection fade out only to be replaced by that of the woman she'd come to know over the course of her life. The woman who visited while Melanie dreamed and who whispered in her ear when danger came--Elizabeth. The woman stood about four inches shorter than Melanie. Her hair was the same shade of blonde. They looked like cousins or even sisters. Lifting her hand, Melanie watched as the image of Elizabeth did the same exact thing. Melanie moved again and Elizabeth's reflection mirrored her.

Green drew in a ragged breath as he stared at the mirror, too.

Ferdian laughed and the sound made her shudder. "It's funny how things work out, Melanie. That is what you prefer to be called now, right? I can understand why. I should have seen it. All those years of sensing her near you but never finding her, even though the path of her magik was fresh. I thought it odd I'd lose Elizabeth's trail completely a little over fifty years ago and then suddenly find it again twenty five years later. Yet, no matter how many times I came looking, I only found you, Melanie. You, the little defiant girl who knew words bigger than she should and things about me that only my wife knew."

"For the love of dick, like you being an asshole is some national secret," she said, instantly wishing she hadn't.

Ferdian winked and she slid closer to Green. He wrapped his arm around her protectively, while still on his knees, and the look Ferdian shot him scared Melanie. She decided to divert his attention from the fact she found Green's embrace safe and didn't want him harmed.

"How are you doing that? How are you making me see Elizabeth in the mirror?"

Ferdian appeared caught off guard. He stood tall, eyeing her suspiciously. "Wait, are you telling me you don't know you're her?"

"*Pfft*, spooky and certifiable. Wonderful." She gave him a drool look. "I'm like four inches taller than her, have blue eyes, not light gray and," she tossed her hands in the air, "why am I explaining that I'm not two people? That's impossible. Your faerie dust must be tainted or something."

A deep laugh tore free from him as he ran his finger over the mirror. "Oh, Elizabeth, Medrawd was wise to build a wall between your essences to keep me from fully sensing you. I should have guessed. After all, Medrawd was like a father to you, the only family you ever really knew. It makes sense you would be born unto him, to hide under his watchful eye."

She arched a brow. "Did you just go insane or is this a recent development? I mean, you've always been creepy but now you're mental to boot."

He licked his lips. "Oh, I very much wish to play with your new body. You're right. It is taller than your other. I have to admit the resemblance while very similar is different enough to throw me. So much of Tatiana is in you now. She must have been thrilled to know her best friend had been given a second chance through the child she and Medrawd brought into the world."

The low, animalistic growl that came from Green startled her. Melanie refused to allow Ferdian to know how much she valued Green's safety so she did her best to ignore him.

"Leave my mom out this, dickhead. If my father hates you, I can only imagine what my mother thinks of you." A shiver of disgust moved over her. "Never mind, I just got a pretty good idea."

He chuckled. "Tatiana helped you escape me, didn't she?"

Melanie shook her head. "Earth to crazy guy who used to live under my bed, I have no clue what you're talking about. Why would my Mom need to help me escape anything? Well, once she helped me sneak out to go to a school dance. My Father had figured out I'd been sneaking out behind his back, flipped and threatened to put bars on my windows."

Missy chuckled nervously. "He did put bars on your windows."

"Yeah, but not until after I got caught in the backseat of a Chevy making out with that one guy. What was his name?"

"Oh, you're really going to have to be more specific," Missy said. "You were caught doing that a lot."

"Show me that which I seek. That which she hides even from herself and all around." Ferdian waved his hand in the air and the mirror's images began to move on its own. Melanie watched as it showed Elizabeth in long, white flowing robes that somehow managed to form to her petite frame. She turned and Melanie covered her mouth when she saw the bruises and cuts on Elizabeth's face, neck and upper body. They were deep, angry purple and looked painful.

Another woman rushed into the image. Melanie's eyes widened. "Mom? Why is my mother with Elizabeth?"

Ferdian shrugged and tapped the frame. "It is your memories we're viewing. You tell me. Better yet, listen and see for yourself, Melanie *Elizabeth* Daly."

Melanie watched as her mother wrapped her arms around Elizabeth. "You must let me summon Medrawd. You are wrong. He can stop Ferdian. I know he can."

Elizabeth's bottom lip trembled. "I command legions of warriors and was born to control him but I cannot. He will destroy my brother, you, everyone if he suspects you know the truth."

"He is no man, to strike his wife, to do what he has done to you shows his soul is black. We will all come together and fight him. He will not touch you again. I cannot believe you would spend so many years hiding this from me, from your brother."

Elizabeth sighed. "I grow tired of waking each day. I loathe opening my eyes to see him next to me and I wish each time he locks our chamber room door it will be the time he loses that last bit of control. I wish for death, Tatiana, yet it never comes." Closing her eyes, Elizabeth let magik move over her, rapidly healing the bruises and wounds. "He has forever to lock me in his hell. Forever to...." She stopped and tipped her head to the side. She gasped. "That is it, Tatiana. Forever. If I take it from him, he has nothing to hold me to him."

"Take it from him?" Tatiana-drew in a sharp breath. "No! You cannot possibly think to give up your--"

Elizabeth nodded. "My immortality. Yes. It is perfect. I can live among mortals and I can live free of him. Without my magik, my immortality, I am no longer bound by the law of the Fae. I am no longer his wife."

"But you will die."

A lone tear trickled down Elizabeth's cheek. "Tatiana, I would accept death with open arms if it means I am permitted even a minute of freedom, of happiness. Medrawd is good to you, as a husband should be. You do not live in fear that at any moment your husband will come in and decide he does not like the way you are looking at him. I only wondered why he was covered in blood, Tatiana. That is all. He took it as a sign I was questioning his decision on the battle field. I was not."

"What did he do to you?"

Elizabeth shook her head. "It matters not. Are you willing to help me be free? Help me find happiness?"

"I would do anything for you. You know that."

She nodded. "Very well, would you be willing to act as guardian for my separable soul?"

"Oh gods, no, Elizabeth, you cannot think I am worthy of guarding your immortality. Let the elders do it. It is part of their function. Allow Medrawd."

"No!" Elizabeth shouted. "My brother must not know of this. He will try to stop me and then he will die at Ferdian's hands. That is not acceptable. Tell him I will contact him when it is safe. I will let him know when I find happiness."

With that, Elizabeth lifted her arms in the air and closed her eyes. "Grant me the knowledge to blend, to live among the mortals and to be one with them. In return, I offer my extended time in good faith."

Light consumed her and in an instant she was standing in a long poodle skirt, a snug pink sweater and a pair of saddle shoes. Her long blonde hair was now bobbed to just below her chin with the slightest of waves to it. She drew in a deep breath. "Do you smell that, Tatiana?"

"No," Tatiana said, through her tears.

"It's mortality. It's freedom."

"But how will you live? How will you survive? You have no family in the mortal realm, no friends."

Elizabeth winked. "Have no fear. I thought of that before I handed over my powers. I will be attending one of those higher schools of learning we happened upon when protecting the humans from the Slothian attack."

"The attack they never knew was taking place? The one that we were supposed to be invisible to the human eye, yet, that one professor seemed to look directly at you?"

Elizabeth nodded. "Yes. But you must promise to cast a spell to forget what you have learned here today. Ferdian will come to you first when he realizes I am gone. And, Tatiana, I am human now. If he finds me, I will not survive even the smallest of blows from him."

"You have my word. Hug me and promise me that you will take care of yourself. That you will find happiness."

"I will. And I shall see you again, in my next time on this earth, dear friend."

The image faded and Ferdian's gaze fell upon her. "You understand I have learned to control my temper, Melanie."

She glared at him. "You understand I don't give a shit if you learned to stand on your head and spit wooden nickels."

The image in the mirror flickered. It showed Elizabeth with her forehead pressed to a white wall. Her stomach was swollen to the point it was obvious she was very pregnant.

Ferdian stood tall and looked as though he'd been struck as he saw it. "No!"

Elizabeth clutched her stomach and cried out. "Something's wrong! Honey," she fell to her knees, "help me, please. The baby, something's wrong with the baby!"

Break the mirror!

Listening to her inner voice, Melanie got to her feet and sent a wad of power at the mirror. It shattered into itself and disappeared. Ferdian drew his hand back and she knew what he was planning on doing. She glared at him. "I don't know what you and Elizabeth had but if you hit me I'll rip your fucking dick off and shove it down your throat."

"You have not the skills or the power." He glared at her. "You are conflicted and even when you were a warrior, feared by others, you had not the skills to stand up to me."

"You fucking son-of-a-bitch!" Green made a move to charge Ferdian and Melanie tossed power around him, pinning him in place. She slapped a silence spell over him and let her instincts take over. Green didn't look pleased but at least he was alive.

She walked straight at Ferdian and took hold of his fist. Ferdian couldn't have looked more surprised if he tried. Leaning into him, Melanie let her voice go soft, breathy and her power to run over her. "I grew up knowing Elizabeth. I know our similarities and I know our differences."

Snapping her fingers, she made the room fill with the sounds of sex. Moans, grunting, sighs and a rhythmic thumping surrounded her. Ferdian glanced around and then at her and she began to sway her body slowly. Melanie moved against him and pressed her lips to his ear. His entire body went rigid and she could sense how horny he was.

She let out a sultry laugh. "See, Ferdian, I know Elizabeth was timid, shy in the bedroom. That her skills were that of a warrior--that of a Valkyrie-like woman. I also know you ruled her with an iron fist and used sex as a weapon. She was scared of sex, of you. I'm not." She nipped playfully at his ear lobe and he actually jerked. "I like it rough, sweet and slow, any way really."

"This is a most welcome addition," he said, his voice cracking slightly.

"Mmmhmm, I bet it is. You always wished she was more aggressive in the bedroom. More willing to express her wants, her desires. More willing to allow you to freely display yours."

He nodded and whimpered as she raked her fingernails down his torso.

"You hated how submissive she was. She didn't make you work at being dominant. She never stood up to you the way you needed her to. Your body craved a woman who would be as strong as you in the bedroom. Someone who would make your body burn even more." She let out a soft laugh. "She didn't but I will."

Melanie kneed him hard in the groin and when he went forward, she thrust her leg up again, hitting him in the face. He went to the floor, clutching himself. She put her hand out. "Gun." One flew towards her and landed lightly in the palm of her hand.

She winked. "I know it won't kill you but I bet it will hurt like hell."

He shook his head. "You do not want me as your enemy."

She laughed. "Hey, cockknocker, I watched the playback. I saw how you were to your *wife*. Fuck yeah, I want you as an enemy. At least that way I know your intentions are purely evil. In truth, it's you who doesn't want me as one."

The only remaining man who had come with Ferdian charged her. She spotted him out of the corner of her eye and waited until he was almost upon her. Giving into what felt natural, Melanie ducked, and the man went up and over her head. He landed at Green's feet.

Melanie watched in awe as Green broke part of her hold on him, seizing hold of the man's head, twisted quickly and then discarded the man's limp body. His hot gaze landed on Ferdian and his mouth moved but her silence spell kept anyone from hearing what was no doubt a threat. It took her a moment to get over the ease in which he killed the man but when she did, she realized she needed to do something about Ferdian and fast.

A trickle of knowledge about Ferdian. She smiled down at him. "I know your weakness, Ferdian."

His gaze shifted as something dark moved over his face. "You are my only weakness."

"Yeah, someone just sort of whispered that in my ear. Guess what else they told me?"

His jaw clenched. "What?"

"Medrawd still hates you." Bending down quickly, Melanie slammed her hand on the ground. "Daddy! Daddy!"

The room crackled with power and in an instant her father stood next to her. He looked at her, not looking a day older than when she was a little girl. The minute his gaze fell to the gun in her hand, his brow furrowed. It went to Ferdian next. His eyes widened and then narrowed. "I told you to *never* set foot near my daughter again."

Ferdian put his hands up and smiled innocently. She wasn't buying it. Even spread out on the lobby floor, he still managed to appear threatening. Part of her knew he could level the place with nothing more than a thought but she also knew he wouldn't. Not yet anyway. As his blue-gray eyes shifted in her direction, his smile took on a sinister vibe. "We shall meet again, Melanie."

A brilliant white light bathed the room, temporarily blinding all present. Something brushed past Melanie and it took her a moment to realize it was Ferdian. His lips crashed down on hers and he stole a kiss before she could comment. His tongue skated over hers and a tiny portion of her body responded to his touch. It was as though the Fae within her recognized another. It had happened before, whenever she took a Fae lover to her bed but something in her also seemed to recognize Ferdian as a threat. As the light disappeared, so did all traces of Ferdian.

Everything that had transpired seemed to slam into Melanie all at once. The reality of it all was too much for her to bear. She looked at her father, instantly felt like a child again and dropped the gun as tears filled her eyes. "Daddy."

In a heartbeat, he had his large arms wrapped around her. He'd always seemed larger than life to her. In many ways he was. He easily stood six five or so and had always had the physique of a warrior. Though her father had been nothing but gentle and loving to her and her brother, Melanie knew he was capable of defending his family. She also knew that part of him missed the days of old, when he'd battle things she couldn't even begin to imagine. "Oh, baby, you're freezing. Eadan!"

The air in the room grew heavy once more before a crackle sounded. Suddenly, Eadan appeared next to her. "Mels?" He looked around the room, letting his gaze rake over the bodies scattered throughout. "Holy shit, Missy, did you go on a killing rampage and not invite me along to watch? Hey, you aren't supposed to be doing anything now that you're expecting."

Missy snorted. "No, your baby sister did."

"No way," Eadan said, his voice barely there as shock etched his face. For a moment, it appeared as if Eadan were moving through molasses as he rounded on her. Never in her life could Melanie remember a time when her brother looked so dumbfounded.

Melanie's father drew in a sharp breath. "Did Ferdian see her attack the men?"

"Yes," Missy said, her voice barely above a whisper.

He grabbed Melanie's shoulders gently. "Did you use your power in front of him? Did he ask you about Elizabeth again?"

"I killed people. I shot ... oh gods, Daddy. I did this. I took lives." She tried and failed to draw in a deep breath. The horror of it all was too great. "How did I do this, Daddy? I've never hurt anyone like this before. Never. I ... I...."

"I know, sweetheart." He stroked her cheek. "If you drew upon the knowledge of how to do this then I fully believe you had no other choice. You are not a violent person, Melanie. This had to be done."

A crazed laugh fell from her lips. "I'm going insane. This can't be real, Daddy. Ferdian isn't real. I don't know how to fire a gun, let alone kill someone." She clung to him, desperate for him to agree, to tell her it was all just a dream. "Daddy, please, I want to wake up and have it all go away. I'm not like this." Lifting her hands, she stared at them in horror as she thought about what they were capable of. They trembled and bile rose in her throat. "I'm going to be sick."

"Melanie," her father whispered. He pushed a piece of her hair back and behind her ear. "Sweetheart."

Shaking her head, she fixated on the dead bodies. Never in her waking hours had she ever seen such carnage. Knowing she was the cause would be her undoing. "Daddy," her lips shook as tears streaked down her cheeks, "I'm a monster. I did this. I killed--"

"Melanie Elizabeth, look at me."

She obeyed. He snapped his fingers and the bodies disappeared, leaving no trace of anything having been out of the ordinary. Her Father was calm on the outside but she could almost see his inner hysteria. "I've no doubt you did what was necessary. But, did you use your powers in front of Ferdian? Was he present when you took the enemy out, Melanie?"

Reluctantly, she nodded. "Yes. He was going to kill them all, Daddy. He wanted to kill the men and take Peren and Missy somewhere other than where he planned on taking me. I could feel their pain as he used his power to try to steal the air from their lungs. The men whom he brought were armed with silver bullets and couldn't wait for a chance to shoot."

"I know, Melanie. I understand how Ferdian operates. He looks for your greatest weakness and uses it against you. He must have sensed your concern for your friends. Did anything else odd happen? I need to know the details, sweetheart, and I know you'd rather not talk about it anymore but this is important."

Melanie's mind raced with thoughts of what had transpired while Ferdian was present. "He had a big gold-edged mirror. It came out of thin air, like how Eadan can conjure various things. It acted like a television and it played something with Mom and Elizabeth in it."

Her father's face fell. "Did it show you in it to start and then...."

"Morph into Elizabeth's image? Yes. Why?" She winced as pain shot through her. Every muscle in her body cramped to the point she drew into herself. "Daddy, something's wrong with my power. It's clawing at me from the insides and I can't make it stop."

Melanie coughed and more blood came up. Her father spotted it and gasped. "Melanie, sweetheart, what's wrong? What happened? Did he hurt you?"

"Dad, pick her up. I'll tell you all about it back at the house," Eadan said, glancing back at the others.

"You will tell me now! What's wrong with my baby?"

Missy rushed up next to Melanie. "Mr. Daly, don't yell at Eadan. He's not trying to keep the truth from you on purpose. He doesn't want to upset Melanie. She's already upset enough."

"Yeah, calling Green 'Thaddy' and shooting me right before you take on a room full of bad guys, while wearing a designer dress, will take it out of you," Wilson said, sliding up next to Missy and touching Melanie's arm.

"Thaddy?" her father asked. "Did you say Green? As in Dr. Thaddeus Chandler Green?"

Wilson laughed. "Ohmygod, your middle name is Chandler? Ha! Ohmygod, she named her baby doll that. This is great. Hey, why aren't you talking or moving?"

Melanie grabbed her father's hand, pushing the pain aside and dropping her hold on Green. "Thad? Is he hurt?"

"Melanie, Thad is dead. I told you that when you were little. He lived a long time ago and is gone now. Do you understand? We went over it hundreds of times. I thought you understood, sweetheart." He sighed and shook his head. "You weren't supposed to remember. You were supposed to let that pain go and start again. A clean slate. That's what I wanted for you."

Eadan gasped. "Oh fuck, Thaddy? The imaginary friend? Chandler, the baby doll's name?" He stared down at Melanie and his eyes widened. "You really are his mate."

Her Father cleared his throat. "Mate? No. Dr. Green is dead. I looked for him after I received the last letter from my sister and found records of his death."

Eadan tapped their father's shoulder. "Umm, Dad, uh, Green is one of the I-Ops. You know the ones Missy's Dad oversees. The ones I'm a part of now. The ones I told you are planning a nice little trip to South America that I want to take Melanie on."

Melanie watched as her father's eyes swirled with varying shades of the blue spectrum. She shook her head and grabbed his arm. "Daddy, no killing Eadan!"

"I'm not going to kill Eadan. I'm going to kill *Dr. Green*. After all, turnabout is fair play. He had a hand in taking you ... umm ... someone close to me once. I think it's only fair I return the favor."

Eadan scrambled next to Melanie and blocked their father's path. "Dad, if you kill Green then you kill Melanie, too. She can't survive without him."

Puzzled, Melanie glanced at her brother and rolled her eyes. "You are such an idiot."

"Yeah, this coming from a woman who worships shoes."

"Yes, well at least my shoes are married to someone else." She glanced behind her at Roi and smiled. "Someone who could kick the living shit out of you."

Roi laughed. "I like her."

"You would," Eadan said drolly. "Put some clothes on Melanie, that dress barely covers you."

"Yes, and the dental floss your last little girlfriend had on covered oh so much more. Bite me."

"Dad, I'm going to wring her neck!"

"You will not touch her. You will, however, point me in the direction of this Green character."

Melanie went to comment but doubled over as pain ripped through her insides. Her Father was on her in an instant. "Sweetheart?"

"Green! Help her, please! I'm sorry I yelled at you. I was wrong. Please," Peren called out, dropping next to Melanie. "Mr. Daly, he needs to touch her and Eadan is right, if you kill Green, you kill Melanie. I think you understand how mating works."

He shook his head. "Peren, tell me that she didn't do it again. Tell me she didn't marry him again. I can't lose her again. I can't."

"*Again?* Dad?" Eadan asked. "Mel has never been married before. Hell, we're excited when she keeps a boyfriend longer than a week."

Chapter Six

Green made his way to Melanie's side slowly, afraid he was dreaming. This couldn't be real. No. It was impossible. As he glanced down at her, her father looked up at him and shook his head. "Tell me she didn't do it again."

"Is she...?" He couldn't get the words out. So many things overlapped. He didn't want to believe it was true. The second he realized that it didn't matter, that he couldn't let Melanie die, regardless who she was or wasn't, his entire body burned for the change.

"Did you kill your wife, Doctor?" he asked.

Green swallowed hard and nodded. "Yes."

Lukian pushed between Green and Melanie's father. "Mr. Daly, what Green is trying to tell you is that he blames himself for her death. He didn't know. None of us knew mortal women couldn't carry our children. He loved her with all his heart, sir. I watched him sit there, powerless as she lost her battle with death. They loved each other so very much."

Medrawd closed his eyes. "Can he fix my daughter?"

"Is she really Elizabeth?" Lukian asked.

Green pushed past him and dropped down next to Melanie. "It doesn't matter! Melanie, honey." He cupped her face as she coughed up more blood. "Honey, look at me."

She did but blinked rapidly. He could sense her pain and wished more than anything to take it from her. Green would gladly suffer to assure himself Melanie was well.

"I can make you better but I need your permission to do something." He drew in a deep breath and let it out slowly. "You have to give yourself to me willingly--agree to let me claim you as my own."

A confused look came to Melanie's face as she curled up into a tiny ball. A whimper broke free from her and Green's chest tightened. "Melanie." He bent down and pressed his lips to hers, giving her a chaste kiss. Heat flared between them and he couldn't help but taste her blood. The animal in him surged forward, ready and willing to claim Melanie for its own. To do what it had never done before, bite a woman, mark her and keep her for all eternity.

Her power erupted, slamming into him and everyone around him. It knocked Green backwards and clear of Melanie's body. He glanced to his side and found Medrawd reaching for him. The man seized hold of Green's upper arm and Green thought for sure he'd attack.

He didn't.

The second Medrawd made contact with him, the feel of Melanie's power lessened before fading away. Green blinked and found himself standing in an open grassy field with Medrawd at his side.

"Doctor?"

Green glanced at him. "What's happening?"

The man stared around at their surroundings and laughed. "Oh, trust her to send us here."

"What?"

"Melanie Elizabeth," Medrawd lifted his hands and motioned towards the far edge of the field.

Green's breath caught as he spotted Elizabeth standing there in a white dress. It clung to her, showing off her form. A form Green had spent one year of his life memorizing. As he stared at her, he couldn't help but think of Melanie in her slinky silver dress.

He shook his head and blinked.

Medrawd touched his shoulder. "Stop fighting it."

"Fighting what?"

"Your mind wants to see what was, what can never be again. Melanie will never be the Elizabeth you remember. She's a different woman now, stronger in many ways yet extremely vulnerable in others. None of us knew what would happen when we decided to bring her back. We only knew the time had come."

Green stared out at Elizabeth. Her hair was much longer than he remembered it being. "Elizabeth?"

She ignored him, like he wasn't even there and focused instead on Medrawd. "Brother, you made the journey."

"Journey?" Green asked.

Medrawd nodded. "She has brought our essences forth to speak to us on a plane not our own. Think of it as crawling into a corner of Melanie's mind."

He wanted to run to Elizabeth, to sweep her up in his arms and never let her go. In the blink of an eye, she was standing before them. So close, yet he knew without being told that if he dared to touch her, it would all end.

She smiled at Medrawd. "Thank you for answering my call."

"As if you gave me a choice. Will Melanie remember this when she wakes?"

Elizabeth gave Medrawd a soft look. "You mean if she wakes, brother."

Shaking his head, Medrawd staggered backwards a bit before sinking to his knees. "No, I can't lose you both. I can't. She's my baby girl. My...."

"Medrawd, you're doing it again. You're separating us and that belief only makes it harder for her to fight--to come to terms with me, with who we are."

He kept his head down. Green didn't. He stayed paralyzed, watching what he knew shouldn't be. Elizabeth didn't even glance in his direction. It was as though she didn't even know he was there. She dropped to one knee and sighed. "Medrawd, you are the only father I have ever known."

Medrawd let out a sob and his shoulders shook. "Tell me how to save my baby, Elizabeth. Eadan says she's mated herself to...."

Elizabeth touched Medrawd's cheek. "I'm not ... umm ... Melanie isn't mated to anyone. They have it wrong. Their thoughts are so loud at times it's deafening. I can see why they'd assume the mating process had begun. They also suspect she could be carrying another's child. Some man named Lance. That's not the case. Melanie is a full-blooded Fae. She can only carry her mate's child, no exception. Her mate, regardless what lifetime she's in, is the same. In her case, his soul never left the body she met him in."

Medrawd let out a chocked sob. "Oh gods, that's why you and Ferdian never had a child. You couldn't. He didn't want to listen. He thought you didn't want one. But he wasn't your...."

Elizabeth nodded. "Ferdian was never my true mate. It's not important now. What is important is that Melanie is not with child. She's not mated, nor is she going through withdrawal. What is happening is difficult to overcome. It's not a matter of another swooping in and doing what he feels he should to make it right again. While it will lessen the direct effects of what's happening, it won't stop it. It will only buy a little bit of time."

"What do you mean? What's happening to Melanie?"

"The man she met a few weeks back did the unthinkable. He knocked the protective wall you'd all assured was in place to keep Ferdian from being able to figure out Melanie is me."

Green drew in a sharp breath at the confirmation.

Medrawd shook his head. "That's impossible. We made sure to make it so that it could never be removed--that Melanie would be her own person in addition to having your soul." His breath hitched. "The blood, the fatigue, the weight loss ... she's fighting the merge."

"Yes, by separating us in her mind at such an early age and then reinforcing it again and again, telling her that her memories were wrong, while necessary to keep her--us--safe from Ferdian, it added bricks and mortar to the invisible line that kept a balance of two lifetimes."

"I killed my baby?" Medrawd struck the ground.

Elizabeth shook her head and wrapped her arms around him. "No. It had to be done, Medrawd. Melanie is so strong that from day one she was able to tap into residual memories from our past. Had the original safeguards not been in place, Ferdian would have discovered our secret the day she was born."

She held Medrawd to her. "He would have taken her and kept her from you. Instead, he terrorized her, always sensing the truth but never being able to put his finger on it. Of course, it helped that at such a young age, any memory she had she assumed was like a movie, a larger than life play. She plucked through and found pieces of things no one thought she could. Think about it, Medrawd, she had an invisible friend named Thaddy. A doll named Chandler? A doll she wouldn't let anyone touch. A doll that when you took it from her, doing your best to explain she couldn't take it to school with her, left her devastated for months and months. Do you understand it represented the child I lost? Thad and I had planned to name our son Chandler? That was a memory I did not want her to retain. Yet she did to some degree."

Medrawd shook his head. "I didn't mean to drive a wedge between you. I didn't. She--"

"Was tapping too far into her past life to be safe in this one. She felt the desperate need to hold a baby and hold onto to the idea of a man she knew as safe, as someone larger than life who would love and protect her, a man who in her first life she did not suspect was an immortal until it was too late."

Medrawd stared up at her. "Gods, you knew the minute you passed on that Green was an immortal that's why Melanie asked for him non-stop when she was little. She knew he was still alive. He's here, Elizabeth."

"I know. I can feel him holding my hand right now, in the reality from which I stripped you from. I'm lying on the floor and he's next to me. His heart is big but I won't let him do what he was trying to do. I won't let him claim me."

"You mean Melanie, right?"

She sighed. "Medrawd, you don't understand--we are one. Melanie and I are the same person regardless if our exterior has changed. I'm the portion of her psyche that she has been raised to believe is her friend Elizabeth, the one who visits at random times when she looks in the mirror or when she's sleeping. I can understand what's happening. The part that's new, the part you think of as Melanie can't comprehend the idea of having lived another life and, to be honest, that was for the best. It meant Ferdian couldn't understand it either but the minute a man showed up in a bar reminding her of someone she once knew, the walls between the essences began to crumble."

Medrawd covered his mouth. "She's doing it to herself?"

"Yes. In the last two weeks the wall that had been so solid that I even believed for a moment we were two separate beings literally exploded. Power, magik she can't even begin to understand is ripping at her system, fighting to keep what was the same. Her inner safeguards tell her that something deadly, Ferdian and the others, will come for her, for the ones she loves if she dares give in but if she doesn't, she will die. She can't be forced to accept who and what she is, has been and will be. It won't work. It's something she has to come to terms with on her own."

"Green could make her understand, right? I mean if you're the same then she'll listen to him."

Elizabeth laughed. "Are you the same man you were four hundred years ago, Medrawd?"

"Yes."

"Oh, really? Then why are you here with me? Shouldn't you be out creeping into the windows of young maidens you wish to bed before you accidentally stumble upon your mate? Shouldn't you be out fighting in the Fae wars? Shouldn't you be with Ferdian? The two of you were best of friends."

He jerked back. "No! I would never do that. I love Tatiana and have been nothing but faithful to her since the day I met her. And I hate Ferdian with a ... oh, okay I get it. You've changed, or rather, Melanie has. She won't listen to Green like you would have. I failed you."

Elizabeth sighed. "Brother, look at me. You are the only father I have ever known. Do you think I would have allowed myself to be brought back to anyone other than you?"

Medrawd hugged her tight. "How can I help her ... umm ... you?"

Something rustled in the tree line. Green turned to find Melanie rushing through. She ran straight for Medrawd. "Daddy? Elizabeth?"

Medrawd pushed to his feet and pulled Melanie into a hug. "Fight this, sweetheart."

Melanie's brow furrowed. "Umm, Daddy? You're squeezing too tight."

"Sorry." He loosened his hold on her. "I'll leave the two," he glanced at Green, "of you to talk." With that, he disappeared.

It was then Green knew for certain that the women couldn't see him standing there.

Elizabeth stood slowly. "What is it? What are you sensing?"

Melanie arched a brow. "Anyone want to tell me where we are and why you two were hugging? Better yet, don't. My head feels like mush right now anyway." She smiled wide and ran to Elizabeth. The minute she tossed her arms around her the two seemed to merge into one person.

Green gasped.

For a split second, only Melanie stood before him. The minute they broke their embrace, Elizabeth stood there as well. Melanie smiled. "You know, it's funny we'd bump into each other again. I've been having the absolute craziest dreams with you in them at random times throughout the day, and I had a run in with your ex."

Elizabeth smiled. "Melanie, I need for you to listen close to me. Remember how I taught you to help keep me hidden from Ferdian?"

Melanie nodded.

"I need you do it again, only this time, when you're somewhere safe, do the opposite."

Puzzled, Melanie's brow furrowed. "I don't understand." She waved her hand in the air. "It doesn't matter. I was going to try to reach you later anyway. I have to ask you something. You're looking like you're about to do the read my mind thing again."

Elizabeth sighed. "Yes, Melanie, I know Green seems familiar to you but I need you to stay away from him. I need you to promise to never see him again. Do you hear me? Never again."

Green's stomach tightened as he heard the words fall from Elizabeth's lips.

"Why?" Melanie asked.

Elizabeth closed her eyes. "Many reasons. One, I'm not sure he has it in him to see me ... umm ... you for you now and not a memory he's clung to for fifty years. You will never be happy in that situation. Ever. Neither will he. For another thing, Ferdian will kill him because Thad will try to stop him from taking you. Thad can't win against Ferdian. No one can."

Melanie gasped. "No! I won't let Ferdian hurt Green. I'll stop him."

"No! Melanie, every time you stand up to Ferdian, every time you tap into the ancient power you carry you tip him off as to how powerful you are. You give him clues as to what your weaknesses are. He's evil to the core. I've explained that to you already."

Melanie put her hand on her hip. "You know, I've spent my life coming to you for advice when I'm scared or confused yet here you are acting like the stupidest woman ever created in the face of something or rather, someone, who scares you."

Elizabeth's eyes widened. So did Green's.

"Do you honestly think Ferdian will leave the men on Lukian's team alone? I saw the way he looked at Green in there. He knows I care about him and he wasn't happy about it. Do you think he'll crawl back under the bed and stay there? You sugar coat things, Elizabeth. You always have, like I'm too delicate compared to you to take the truth." Melanie bent down and tapped nothing, before throwing her voice to sound like Elizabeth's. "Sweetie, he's got a black heart. He's evil to the core."

Melanie threw her hands in the air and shook her head. "The man is a Fae deity of death and destruction. Call a spade a spade!"

Elizabeth covered her mouth. "How do you know what type of Fae he is?"

"Oh, I don't know. I just do. I also know why you hid from him. I've always known. But I thought he wasn't real. Evil doesn't begin to cover it, Elizabeth. The man is sick in the head. Seriously fucked! I can see how you'd fall for his charms at first. I know he has them because I felt myself starting to fall for them, but to do that you...."

Elizabeth stopped short of touching Melanie. "When you wake, the others will ask about Ferdian. They'll want details as to how you know him, who he is, so on and so forth. Don't tell them. Not even Peren or Missy. Their mates can read them and they'll tell Green."

Melanie sighed. "Elizabeth, do you really think I'd tell them that bastard spent decades raping and torturing you? I know how hard it was for you to break the cycle, to get out and keep your family and friends safe. I know what you gave up and I know that you wouldn't change it for the world. Your time as a mortal made up for all the years of living in fear of the man. I also know you learned in death that you always had the power to stand up to Ferdian and he knew it. It's why he ruled you with an iron fist."

Anger rose in Green, making him want to shift and rip something to pieces as he heard the things Elizabeth had kept hidden from him. Ferdian would die. Green would see to it.

"Melanie, don't you dare think of taking him on! He will kill you in an instant. We aren't merged fully and you aren't strong enough ... oh gods ... I'm not strong enough to face him again. I can't look at him and look Green in the face. I can't."

"Oh, that is bullshit! If Green is the type of man who would look at a woman who was raped differently, then he isn't someone you need in your life."

Elizabeth laughed and it sounded so out of place. "It's moments like this I find myself thinking like Medrawd--that we're separate when we're not. I spent all those years as a woman that men feared coming after, yet, I feared something too, or rather, someone. I spent my life wishing for a non-violent man. A man who--"

"Wouldn't raise his hands and strike you but rather use them to play you the most beautiful songs on the piano." Melanie nodded. "Yeah, I know. I, umm, hell, I even found myself craving that. I got shot down and told to stop reading the guy I asked but, oh, well. Though, I wasn't reading him. I swear. I just sort of know things about him."

Guilt tore through Green as he stared at Melanie. She'd made a simple request and he'd treated her poorly.

She let out a soft laugh as tears filled her eyes. "Now, you know why I don't open up to men. Why it's easier for me to just take what I want and discard them. They're good for sex and that's it. If I need to talk to someone, I call my friends. Hurts less when they treat me like shit."

Another pang of guilt ripped through him.

Elizabeth closed her eyes and shook her head. "I'm so sorry, Melanie. I didn't mean to do this to you."

"Do what?"

"Make you think there is no such thing as love. Make you into someone who has had to spend her entire life hiding the inner you. Someone who goes out of her way to avoid emotional attachments to the opposite sex. I'm so sorry."

Melanie looked up and reached for Elizabeth. "You need to hide, like now! Ferdian's power is in the air around me."

"Swear to me that you won't try to fight him and that you'll stay away from Green," Elizabeth said, sounding panicked. "You aren't strong enough to fight them both, Melanie. One has the power to destroy you physically and the other can do it emotionally."

Melanie stood tall. "You've always told me that I couldn't go up against a man like Ferdian. That he'd destroy me."

"He will. Men feared me. I walked among a league of Fae warrior women who can only be compared to the Amazon or the Valkyries and even I wasn't strong enough to defeat him."

Melanie smiled. "Here lies the biggest difference between us, Elizabeth. My mother comes from a very long line of Fae that can only be associated with nymphs, sirens, and any other kind of seductive temptresses. She told me once that was why she was my father's mate, his wife, because only someone like her could tame his wild streak. I may need your help understanding how to fire a weapon but I don't need your help when the weapon is sex."

Elizabeth lunged for Melanie but Melanie side stepped her. "No! Don't you dare try to get past his defenses by seducing him. He'll destroy you."

"I'm dying. I know that. Might as well take the boogieman down with me. Now," Melanie tipped her head back, "I think it's time you hide."

"I need to tell you how to wake us up," Elizabeth said.

"No. I don't want your help. Not if you're willing to turn your back on Green. I won't let Ferdian hurt him. Green may think the worst of me but I think he's a great man. I refuse to push him aside and leave him to fend for himself."

Power surged around Green and he blinked to find himself staring at Melanie. She was lying on the floor next to him. His hand was wrapped in hers. Medrawd was bent over her, touching her cheek.

He looked at Green and sighed. "She's fighting to come to now. I'm holding her back because she fully intends on erasing everyone's memory of what transpired."

Green lifted a brow. "She can do that?"

"Oh, yes. Though, I didn't realize I'd passed it onto her until Missy's father called me one day when they were teenagers, demanding to know why she wasn't grounded for getting caught sneaking out again when the other two girls were up shit creek. He told me that I'd been furious but for some reason, I kept letting Melanie off." He chuckled. "It was then I figured out I'd passed the gift to erase short-term memories to her. You'll be immune to it.

It's not something Elizabeth could do so I didn't expect Melanie to be able to do it either."

"You're responsible for me seeing what went on, aren't you?" Green asked, keeping his hand around Melanie's.

"You had a right to know the truth. If what Lukian said is true, that you loved her and she you, then I owed you as much." He ran a hand through his hair, clearly shaken. "I thought if you understood you might be able to help me figure out a way to save my daughter. You see, she will either kill herself with her own power, merge fully with her other essence, or...."

"Or?" Green was sure he didn't want to hear what Medrawd had to say but he didn't have a choice.

Medrawd swallowed hard. "Or Melanie or Elizabeth's personality, their essence, will figure out a way to survive independent of the other. Meaning, we could end up having Elizabeth without Melanie's memories or vice versa. I love my sister, Green. My daughter, however, is my daughter. I don't want to lose either but it may come to that. I know you have nothing to gain if Melanie is the one who comes through, and to be honest, I can't see Elizabeth or Melanie willingly fighting the other to survive. It's confusing I know. I won't blame you if you walk away and wash your hands of this. I think that's what Elizabeth would prefer you do."

Green held tight to Melanie. "Yes, but Melanie doesn't want to push me away and I don't want to go."

"I can't hold her back anymore. I've given her what strength I can without overloading her system. She has no clue you were there, Green. And the others won't remember seeing her do what she did in front of Ferdian. They won't even remember meeting him. I can feel his power lingering. He's monitoring what she's doing. Now that he knows the truth, he will stop at nothing to have her back. I'll do my best to keep an open line with Melanie. Ferdian is powerful enough to cut me off from her, though."

He nodded. "We'll be fine. Do what you need to. I'll find a way to destroy him." He held Melanie's hand tight.

Medrawd kissed Melanie's cheek. "Happy Birthday, sweetheart."

"Wait! Tell me why she keeps her birthday a secret."

Medrawd sighed. "Because it's the same day she died, Green. It was this day all those years ago that she died trying to give birth to your son. We had no choice but to bring her back on the same day of the year. To her, it is not a joyous day. It's a day she feels sorrow. I didn't realize she could tap into memories from her past life and the year she was to turn four, she asked for something for the first time." His eyes glistened. "She asked for a boy baby doll with red hair and green eyes. I couldn't deny my baby girl the only thing she'd ever asked me for. I couldn't." He shook his head. "I should have. From the minute she opened her present, she refused to let it go. By giving her that gift, I didn't know what I was feeding into on her birthday. She no doubt feels the loss of her child and her husband but doesn't understand it. It's always been a day Melanie does her best to hurry through."

Chapter Seven

Green stared at Medrawd, unable to believe what he'd heard. Power surged around Green. He blinked and found himself staring down at Melanie as she stood before him, cuffing the sleeves of his dress shirt. He couldn't help but smile. The point she'd taken them back to was a happy moment for all involved.

She put her hands in his and winked. "Let's dance."

He stood there, soaking in her beauty, amazed with her strength, her courage.

"I'm not allowed to start until you do. You value your toes too much," she said, laughing softly.

Some Enchanted Evening sounded from the other room. "Something tells me that I don't have to worry about that particular body part when it comes to you, Melanie."

Her gaze flickered down him and landed on his groin. His cock hardened instantly. Taking their joined hands, he pulled them to his chest, above his heart. "I was thinking more on this level."

She looked confused. He wasn't surprised. He'd seen her inner struggle. Love wasn't a word that came into play in her current existence. If Green had anything to say about it, it would. The woman in his arms had refused to push him aside, to ignore him. She believed in him and he couldn't help but believe in her as well.

Green positioned himself and launched into the foxtrot with Melanie. When she fell in line with him and didn't immediately step on his foot he knew that while she carried Elizabeth's soul, she indeed had grown, evolved into someone even more perfect than he'd ever dreamt possible.

They moved around the lobby, their gazes locked. The smile Melanie wore was infectious. Green found himself returning it and wagging his brows as he began to sing along with Sinatra. The sheer joy of having her safe and in his arms outweighed any inhibitions he had. It's been over fifty years since he felt the urge to sing. Now, he wanted to shout it off the rooftops that Melanie was his.

Melanie's face lit and Green's heart thumped madly in his chest. As he sang about finding his true love and never letting her go, he pulled her closer to him and swayed her slightly.

Laughing, Melanie kissed his cheek. "Aren't you just full of surprises?"

"You have no idea," he said, dipping her back. "Don't worry, you've shocked me to the core too, honey.'

Their lips brushed and Green's entire body tightened. He went to kiss her but she tipped her head to the side, leaving him kissing her upper neck. A purr emanated from deep within him and Melanie shivered in his arms.

The smell of her arousal filled the air. It took everything in Green not to take her to the floor and sink his cock into her. He pulled her back to a standing position and brought her hand to his lips. Kissing the back of it, he locked gazes with her. "Happy Birthday."

"Huh? I wiped everyone's memories ... uh ... uhh, thank you."

He stilled. He hadn't given any thought to her wanting to avoid having her friends celebrate her birthday. He waited with bated breath for her to catch on that he'd not been affected by her memory spell.

The band changed songs and Melanie grabbed his hand. She pulled him quickly through the restaurant, past Lukian and the others, directly towards the stage. The house band nodded and winked at her as she led Green to a chair at a table up front. "My turn to, I hope, surprise you."

She'd already more than done that but he nodded all the same.

Melanie took the hand of the trumpet player and climbed onto the stage. Peren came rushing up with Missy close behind her. "Holy shit, she's going to actually do it in front of a crowd?"

Peren laughed. "I better warn Lukian and the rest of the guys that this place is going to turn into horny men central in about two seconds." She paused and looked down at Green. Her brow furrowed. "I feel like I owe you an apology but I'm not sure why."

He smiled and winked. "Grab your husband and join me."

She nodded.

Directing his attention to the stage, Green's eyes widened as he watched Melanie begin to dance to the sound of *All That Jazz*. She moved like a flapper from the twenties, like a pro. She was not only sexy and breathtaking but talented as well.

She arched her brows and locked gazes with him as she grabbed a microphone. The second she began to sing, his already hard cock dug at his pants, wanting to be free, to be in her. Her voice was sultry, just like her.

Jon and Wilson moved up and stood to the side of Green. "Whoa," Wilson whispered, as Melanie slid a hand down her body seductively while hitting the bluesy notes. "Umm, Green, if you decide you don't want to claim her, can I?"

Chancing a glance at Wilson, he found the man staring dreamily up at the stage. That wasn't very shocking. What did take him by surprise was the fact that Jon seemed just as riveted. Jon nodded. "Yeah, what he said."

Green couldn't help but chuckle. "Gentlemen, stop ogling my wife."

"Wife?" Roi asked, sliding into the seat next to him. He pulled Missy down onto his lap. "You're going to claim her then?"

He watched her singing and dancing and nodded. "If she'll have me, then, yes, I'm claiming her."

Roi snorted. "Like she has a choice. Without you, she dies." Missy growled. Roi cleared his throat. "You know what I mean."

"She has a choice and I intend to let her make it," Green said, knowing the truth but feeling no need to clue everyone else in on it just yet.

Wilson sat down on the other side of him and patted Green's shoulder. "Green, is it me or does she seem tailor made for you? If they tell me she's a closet geek, I'm grabbing a shotgun and forcing the marriage."

He stared up at Melanie with a smile on his face. "Yeah, she does seem tailor made." Getting to his feet, he glanced down at Wilson. "Save my seat."

"Why? Where are you going?"

"To spend as much time with my mate as I can. I want to convince her to go to South America with us. If I'm lucky and she accepts me, I fully intend on making her understand that I don't care who she is, only that she is my mate."

"Your mate?" Wilson asked. "You don't really think she's your...." He stopped short of finishing his sentence and glanced up at Melanie. "Whoa."

"Yeah, whoa," Jon said, going to sit down but missing the seat and falling on his ass.

Lukian and Roi laughed. "Whatever you're going to do, you better do it soon or these two morons will be trying to win her hand."

He glanced back at his long-time friend. "Captain, they're welcome to try but I should warn you and them that I can and will kill for her. Friend or foe."

Lukian drew his mate into his arms. "As it should be, Green. It's good to see you smile again. It's been a long time."

"Too long," Green said as he headed straight for Melanie.

The restaurant erupted into applause as she drew the song to an end. Her eyes locked on his and he put his arms up to her. Melanie stepped into them and he eased her off the stage. The very feel of her body pressed to his left his cock straining and the desire to come great. Even more than that, it left his heart thumping madly for the woman he held.

Chapter Eight

Melanie went to open the door of Green's silver Escalade and froze when he put his large hand on her bare upper thigh. He squeezed gently, drawing her attention to him and making moisture pool in the juncture of her thighs. "Umm, thanks for the ride home."

"Melanie, let me take you somewhere else, somewhere nice to spend the rest of your birthday." He glanced at the sport's bar that her family owned and shook his head. "I can hear the music blaring out here. I know your apartment is above it. You aren't getting any sleep with that going on."

She couldn't help but laugh. "Ah, this is the part where I offer to take you up and fuck you. I get it. My reputation precedes me."

He tightened his grip on her thigh. "That's not what I said."

"But it's what you meant." The second she said it, she regretted it. "I'm sorry. You're right. I'm tired and a bit grumpy. It's been a long day." She glanced at him, not wanting to tell him everything that had truly transpired. "A *really* long day. It doesn't help that I woke up wanting it to be tomorrow either."

"Why, wouldn't you want it to be today, Melanie?" he asked, though something in his voice made her wonder if he already knew.

"It's hard to explain, mostly because I'm not even sure why I do. I just know I wish this day could just fall off the calendar." She rolled her eyes playfully even though she wanted to give into the urge to cry.

Green caressed her inner thigh. "Until I met you, this day in particular, was a dark one that I loathed, too. I'd spend it locked away from the rest of the world, drowning in my sorrows. You've made the day a hell of a lot brighter, Melanie."

Confused, Melanie put her hand over his. "Umm, no offense, Green, but the mention of me and brighter days aren't synonymous to most, so excuse me if I inquire as to why they are for you?"

A soft chuckle came from him. "You're doing it again."

"What?"

"Letting the fact you're obviously a very intelligent young woman show through."

Embarrassed, Melanie felt her cheeks reddening. She generally kept that part of herself private. No one would believe her anyway if she confessed to just how intelligent she truly was. They seemed to like putting her into a pre-done mold, where they assumed she was a walking, but empty-headed blonde. "Great, I can stand naked in front of an auditorium full of people and not break my stride. You comment on my having a brain and I want to crawl under the nearest rock."

"Let me take you somewhere special, Melanie. When I suggested we leave the restaurant it was with the intention of giving you a special night to remember." He tugged on her thigh gently. "And I don't mean that in the way you think I do. So, don't get upset with me."

"You know what? I'd like that very much." She laced her fingers through his and laughed. "It's better we avoid sex anyway."

"Really?" he asked, laughing as well. "Why is that?"

Eyeing him carefully, she smiled. "For one thing, you seem like the marrying type. You know, that kind of guy who can't separate sex and other emotions." She couldn't bring herself to say love. The concept was foreign to her.

"Oh, it's that obvious, is it?" He winked. "Any more reasons as to why it's better if we don't ... umm ... you know."

She grinned. "What you're looking for is 'fuck like animals all night long.'"

His cheeks flared pink and he shifted awkwardly in his seat. "Umm, yeah, that."

"I take it you aren't used to a woman who is sexually charged."

Green snickered. "That's putting it mildly. I thought I was used to a woman who was quiet, reserved, gentle, one who wouldn't know the first thing about defending herself. I recently found out I was mistaken. I think she pulled the wool over my eyes."

"That or she didn't want anything to do with having to defend herself. Maybe, she liked knowing she didn't have to be that person anymore. If it was me, I wouldn't want to walk around with a chip on my shoulder. I'd want to laugh, be happy and not worry about anything beyond that." Melanie stared out the window at the bar and sighed. "When I was little, I'd have these nightmares that seemed so real that I'd be terrified to fall back asleep. They were violent. *Very* violent."

She tapped the glass with her free hand. "The only way I can describe it was like I was standing in the center of some Dark Ages epic battle. There were swords, horses, blood and death everywhere. I'd shoot awake and scream for my father. He'd hold me and tell me that I wasn't allowed to have chocolate before bed again." Melanie made a circle in the condensation. "Green, I could almost feel the blood on my hands. Gods, I was so scared and way too young to be dreaming about that kind of death and destruction. Hell, I'm how old now and don't want to experience it."

"Melanie," he whispered.

"I know. They were just dreams and it's clear I have an overactive imagination. At least I stopped trying to convince everyone that your friend could turn into an animal." Melanie squeezed Green's hand. "I'm sorry. I didn't mean to bring him up. I just...."

"Shhh, honey, it's okay to talk about Lance. He was like a brother to me. He gave his life to keep Peren's safe and it's because of him I found you." He eased his hand up her thigh more, sending fire shooting throughout her. "Tell me your other reasons why nothing should transpire between us. I'm sensing there are more."

The man had a way about him that made Melanie's entire body ache for him. She did her best to stay removed but Green made it hard. He made her crave things she'd never dreamt she'd want. A husband. A family. *Happily ever after.*

"Melanie, talk to me."

Giving in, she looked at him. "You scare me, Green. I'm not a one-man kind of gal and I find myself wanting to...." She stopped and looked at their joined hands. "Forget it. Anyway, I have this phobia about getting pregnant. I'd be the world's worst mother. I think we can all agree on that. I've been told on more than one occasion that I don't have to worry about it but I still do. And I get the feeling if you simply sneeze hard in my direction I'd end up with child." She laughed and winked at him. "This is the part where you run. I think like a man most of the time and I want to run for the hills at the mere mention of a family."

Green just stared at her.

She exhaled deeply. "Shit, I didn't mean to make you uncomfortable. I'm not looking to trap you in something. Hell, I'm not looking to trap any man. I just said what I felt. I'm sorry. I didn't think. Ignore me. I'm rambling and still a little bit grumpy."

He chuckled. "Just a bit, huh?"

"You think this is bad, you should see me when my PMS is in full swing. You'd duck and run for cover."

He laughed. "That bad?"

She went to answer and spotted her brother Eadan in the doorway of the bar. He was shoving a tall, well-built man with a head of wavy brown, chin-length hair out of the bar. Her breath caught. "Eadan, no!"

In an instant, she had the car door open and was running in her heels toward her brother as he drew his fist back. She tossed magik up and let it hit him, giving him a mild shove backwards. He glanced up and narrowed his blue gaze on her. "Dammit, Melanie, I told you to stop hanging around this asshole. Hell, I tell you that about every man you have nipping at your heels!"

"Fuck you," Russell, the muscle-bound stud who had apparently been drinking, said, as he charged at Eadan.

Melanie pointed at him. "Enough!"

He glanced out from bloodshot eyes. "Hey, baby, how are you feeling? Your mom told me you were sick. I thought I'd come and make you well again."

"Baby?"

Melanie turned to find Green standing there, staring at Russell like he wanted to kill him. She shook her head, afraid that Russell would hurt Green. Russell wasn't normal. He was Fae and had spent several years in the Service. He could break a human like Green easily. "It's fine. Thank you for a lovely evening, Green."

"Our evening isn't over, Melanie."

Stepping forward, she put herself between Green and Russell.

Russell staggered a bit. "Who the hell is that?"

"You're drunk."

Russell winked. "You're sexy."

Rolling her eyes, Melanie reached for him. "Give me your keys. You're dangerous enough without putting you behind the wheel of a car when you reek of alcohol."

"I could kill him and lessen the risk to society," Eadan said, grinning. "That or I could turn my back and let Green do it."

Melanie gasped. "Russell will kill him!"

Russell took her hand in his. "Mmm, that's right, baby. Now, come on. I miss you. You haven't returned my calls and your watchdog brother hasn't let me in to see you. It's been almost a month since we've spent a weekend holed up, fucking until neither of us could move. My dick is so hard for you I can't stand it. You're addictive, Melanie. I need to be in...."

Melanie threw power at him to shut him up. It hit him in the head and left him blinking. "Whoa, what was that? Eadan, you throwing magik at me?"

She gasped, her gaze flickering to Green. "Umm, drunks say the darnedest things. Magik? Geesh? Crazy talk."

Eadan snickered.

She glared at her brother. "What's so funny?"

"You can't lie worth a shit. Never could."

"Eadan," she said, glaring at him. "I think I should say goodnight to *Green* before we discuss this any further."

"Why?"

Her eyes widened. "Why the hell do you think, dumbass?"

Eadan laughed. "You say the sweetest things. Can I get a hug?"

"I was going to ask for a blow job but I'll settle for a hug, too," Russell said.

In an instant Green was on him, knocking him on his ass with one hit. Melanie screamed and pressed her body to Green's. "Are you just about done hitting people tonight?"

His jaw tightened. "No. Excuse me. I'd like to hit him some more."

"Hitting Wilson is one thing, Russell isn't like him. He's ... umm ... he could hurt you. Please, Thaddy, don't do this."

"Thaddy?" Eadan asked. "Are you back to talking to invisible friends, Mel? Kind of old for that aren't you? You aren't going to start crying about Dad taking your doll again are you?"

"She's talking to me," Green said, his voice deep, his gaze hard. "And no one will ever take anything from Melanie again. I intend to give her everything she's ever wanted and then some."

"Uhh, what?"

"My name is Thaddeus. Melanie is talking to me. And don't ever bring up the baby again. It upsets her." He glanced at her. "It upsets us both. Understood?"

Eadan drew in a sharp breath. "Oh, shit. You really are her mate."

"Déjà vu." Green made a move to go at Russell.

Melanie did the only thing she could think of, she cupped Green's face and captured his mouth with hers. She thrust her tongue in and moaned as heat flared through her. Her power surged and she let it pour into Green. He lifted her off the ground and kissed her with so much passion her inner legs quivered. She didn't want to pull away but knew she had to. Reluctantly, she did just that.

Green held her and she pushed on his shoulders. "Sleep," she whispered, prepared to cradle his large frame with her magik when he fell to the ground. Problem was, he didn't fall. He didn't even blink. "I said, sleep."

A slow smile spread over his handsome face. "Mmmhmm, I heard you the first time, honey."

Her eyes widened. "Why didn't it work? It always works. Always!"

"Always?" he asked, the slightest hint of amusement danced in his emerald eyes.

Pushing free of his hold, Melanie nodded as she went for Russell who was now being held back by Eadan. She wasted no time in pressing her mouth to Russell's and letting her power out. She pulled back. "Sleep."

He dropped to the graveled parking lot.

"Eadan, you could have caught him!"

Eadan laughed. "Yep. I could have but I didn't. I think my new teammate would prefer I didn't help the guy out any."

Green was behind her in an instant, lifting her into his arms again. He turned her to face him and held her suspended off the ground as if she weighed nothing.

"While I appreciate you demonstrating that it does, indeed, always work, I would really rather you not *ever* touch another man again." His fingers skimmed under her breasts. His gaze fell and Melanie's followed suit.

Her flimsy dress had shifted enough that she was now exposing nipple to him. Growling, he closed his eyes and set her down quickly. Melanie reached for him but he stepped away. "Go to your apartment and lock your doors. Eadan...."

"I'll watch over her," Eadan said. "You going to be all right? You know, you could just do it. She needs you, Green."

"If only that were true," he said, putting his back to her. "Go in and lock your door, Melanie. Now."

Melanie shook her head. "What's going on? Thad?"

"Go," he ground out, his voice so deep that it actually shook her.

Unable to stop herself, she took hold of his shoulder and pulled on him. "Please, Thad, don't be like this."

Slowly, he turned his head to face her. His eyes seemed to glow with and swirl with varying shades of green. His chest heaved and for a split second she was sure that his teeth were sharp, animal-like. Images of being with Lance and having him change into something monstrous, something non-human flooded her. Backing up, she bumped into Eadan and screamed.

Immediately, her brother began to radiate a calming energy. "Mel, it's okay."

Her gaze flickered to Green. He looked normal. Nothing was out of place or glowing. She shook her head. "I think I'm starting to hallucinate again."

"How about I have the cook whip something up for you?" Eadan asked.

The last thing Melanie wanted to do was try to eat. She glanced down at Russell and forced a smile to her face. "No. We'll be fine. Thanks though."

"*We'll?*" Green asked.

"Have no fear, Green," she bit out. "I wasn't lumping you in with me. You're free to go. I'll run right in and lock my door when I'm damn good and ready. I don't need you yelling at me and making all kinds of big scary male noises."

Melanie glanced at Eadan. "Will you help me get Russell upstairs?"

"You are not taking him to your place," Green said, his nostrils flaring.

She snorted. "Uh, yeah I am. Who the hell do you think you are? My father? Nope, sorry, got one of those already. Go boss around your buddies."

"Elizabeth, you are not taking another man to your--" Green stopped and glanced at the ground. "I mean, Melanie."

She wasn't sure why his decision to call her by her middle name upset her but it did. Narrowing her gaze on him, she let it go hard. "You don't get to show up in my life and start issuing orders. I don't understand you. You're nice to me one second and then cold as ice the next. If you hate me for something I did or someone I did," she added, noting his jealous streak, "then I'm sorry but I'm too tired to deal with this."

"Mel, umm, can we take a minute here and try to get along?" Eadan asked. "I've been trying to think of a way to tell you this but I'd like to take you on a trip to South America. Missy and Peren are going. The three of you will have fun, I'm sure of it."

She arched a brow. "Don't bother making future plans for me, Eadan. Go. Enjoy yourselves. I have some things here I need to wrap up."

"Wrap up?"

Disgusted and tired of dealing with questions and moody men, Melanie stormed over to Russell. She bent down next to him, kissed the tips of her fingers and then ran them through his wavy hair.

"You're not waking him up and taking him upstairs with you." Eadan made a move for her and she glared at him.

"I don't really want to be alone tonight. Russell may be drunk but he can still help me if Ferdian comes back."

Green growled. She ignored him.

"Who the hell is Ferdian?" Eadan asked, moving up next to her. "Shit, Mel, tell me you don't have some other guy that's going to start showing up at all hours kicking down your door and coming at you because he's pissed you don't want anything more from him than sex."

She shuddered in disgust. "I do not want sex from Ferdian. Trust me. And it's no big deal, umm, Russell will act as a tripwire so to speak. He can sense other...." Melanie stopped, remembering Green was there.

Eadan grabbed her arm and yanked her to her feet. "Are you fucking telling me that you got some guy who is Fae after you? You are, aren't you? Russell can sense other Fae threats and you know that. It's how you know to get him the hell out of your bedroom before Dad or I come into the bar, isn't it? You know Dad will kill him and you know what I think of him."

Melanie nodded her head toward Green. "Other parties are present, dumbass. I'd really rather not have to cast another spell ... uh ... can we talk about this after Green leaves. I'm not strong enough to do this completely alone. Russell will help because for some insane reason he cares about me." She glared at Green. "And he's never once fucked my name up!" Setting her sights back on her brother, she smiled. "You see him as being a drunken asshole right now. He's not that way all the time. Can't you sense his pain, Eadan?"

"Oh, I'm not going anywhere without you," Green said, his voice deep, hard. "And I really don't give a shit about Russell's pain."

Eadan pointed at Green. "I'm with him. Now, get your ass back in his car. You're going home with him tonight. Then, you're heading out with us to South America. Don't think about arguing or I'll knock your ass out with a spell and you'll wake up married to Green. Understood?"

"What? Now you suddenly want me to go home with a man I just met?" She tossed her hands in the air. "I surrender. I'm just going to say this--fuck whoever hears me. If you force me to leave with Green, there is a better than average chance the man will end up dead. I'm getting the sense you kind of like the guy, Eadan. Do you want to see him after someone who is more powerful than Daddy gets a hold of him?"

Eadan stilled. "I don't know any Fae that is more powerful than Dad."

"I do. The man is ruthless. He'll cut down anyone between him and his goal. Don't ask me to sacrifice the man I love just because you like him better than Russell."

There was a collective gasp. Melanie glanced from her brother to Green. Both looked shocked. She shrugged. "*What?* Why are you guys staring at me like that?"

Green looked at Eadan. "Did she just say that she...?"

Eadan nodded. "Never in my life have I heard the girl utter that about any man, other than her father. Well, there was that invisible friend she loved." His gaze shot to Green's. "Whoa. Umm, on the count of three, catch her. This won't hurt her but it'll piss her off when she comes to. One. Two. Three."

Darkness swallowed Melanie as Eadan's power wrapped around her.

Chapter Nine

Melanie woke to the soft sounds of someone playing a piano. She glanced around the large, white room in awe. It was beautiful. The ceiling was vaulted and the windows along the left wall went from the floor up. The bed was bigger than any she'd ever been in and considering the number of beds Melanie had woke to find herself in that was saying a lot. It was still dark out and she wasn't sure how much time had passed.

She glanced down to find herself wearing one of her favorite nightgowns. The light pink silk gown was slit up the side and had spaghetti straps. It was like wearing nothing and she loved it.

Climbing out of the bed, Melanie listened to the sound of the music playing and smiled. She didn't need to be told whose bedroom she was in. She vividly remembered Eadan threatening to put a sleep spell on her. She also remembered his threat--she'd wake up married to Green. The thought had terrified her when he said it. Now, as she headed for the door, all she could think about was being near Green.

She opened the door and stepped out into the large hallway. The sound of music filtered in from the other end so she headed in that direction. The hallway seemed to go on forever, making her wonder how many people lived in the house. The sound of the piano being played grew louder as she approached a large, half-circular staircase. As she headed down it, she spotted Green in what looked to be a formal living room, sitting with his back to her while he played. The room was amazing but nothing compared to the sight of him.

Her breath caught as she stared at him. It was the first time she'd seen him without a shirt on and it hit her just how muscular he was. He looked as though he were chiseled from the same marble of the floor beneath the area he sat in. Perfection. Plain and simple. The dark black wood of the piano he sat at only added to the sleek, streamlined, sensual look Green put out.

The black silk pajama bottoms he wore, rode low in the back, showing that he had dimples just above his ass cheeks. The urge to rush forward and run her hands over him was great. She managed to control it, only slightly as she walked slowly toward him. His head dipped slightly as he played, indicating just how into it he was.

She wasn't familiar with the piece he was playing but she knew enough to know it was full of emotion. Raw. Powerful, like him. Melanie slid her hands over his shoulders and rubbed gently. The feel of his warm skin beneath her fingertips left her drawing in a deep breath, fighting to keep her breathing even.

Green stopped playing and stiffened. "I didn't mean to wake you. I'll...."

Her nipples hardened to pebble-like peaks as they grazed against his back. Melanie put her lips to his ear and kissed it. The urge to bite it was great so she gave in and nipped playfully at it. "Don't stop, please."

His breathing grew shallow and he refused to look at her. "I can't be by you if you're in that and I'm only in...."

Run away. Don't fall for him.

Ignoring her inner voice, Melanie slipped the straps of her nightgown down her shoulders and let it fall to the floor in a silken puddle. She lifted it with her foot and plucked it from her toe. She let out a sultry laugh as she dropped it in Green's lap.

"There. Problem one out of the way. You take yours off and we'll have everything worked out."

Green stared down at the nightgown and put his hands out on the piano top. He bowed his head and it was easy to see him straining. The fact his knuckles were turning white only added to the matter. "Melanie, I can't fight the beast in me forever. It wants to claim you for its own. I want to claim you, too."

"Well, I've never heard a man refer to the urge to fuck me quite that way but I'm game if you are, Thad."

He shook his head. "No. You don't understand. Hell, I don't even understand it. I controlled the beast easily when we were together before. Never once did I have to push you away to keep from marking you, from sinking my teeth into your smooth skin as I sank my cock deep within you. I was able to keep that side of myself from you. Why now? Why can't I control it around you now?"

Her brow furrowed as she slid her hands into his dark red hair. "Honey, I think the sight of you makes my brain fuzzy because you're not making any sense to me. I keep fighting this nagging voice in my head that's telling me to run. To avoid you at all costs. You scare me, yet when I woke to find myself in your bedroom, I was upset you weren't there with me."

"Melanie, I won't tie you to me. You don't really want that. There is no way I can be with you and keep the beast caged. Please put your clothes back on and give me some time to be alone."

"How long was I asleep?" she asked, biting back tears as he rejected her.

"About two hours, why?"

Two hours? That meant it was still technically her birthday. Barely, but it counted. The irony wasn't lost on her. "You were my bright spot on this day, too," she whispered, low enough a human couldn't hear her. "Okay, I'm going to go lay back down for awhile. I'll see you in the morning."

Reaching out, she went to grab the nightgown and yelped when Green caught her wrist. He drew her into his arms and onto his lap before she could even blink. "Thad?"

His eye seemed to flicker with varying shades of emerald. "Don't be afraid of me, Melanie. I can't control it around you."

She knew she should be terrified of what she was seeing but the feel of his hands on her body left her hissing out as she tipped her head back. "I want you inside me."

"Melanie."

She shifted on his lap, and swung one leg around so she was left straddling him. The feel of his hard erection just beneath the surface of his pajama bottoms spurred her onward. Green closed his eyes and moved his hands off her.

"I can't do this. I can't be gentle with you. It's been over fifty years since I've had sex and even then I didn't have to fight the urge to claim you on a supernatural level."

Fifty years? Supernatural level?

Images of Lance turning into something animal-like while she was with him flooded back to her. Her mind said run. It wanted her to put as much distance between them as possible. Her heart, which never chimed in when it came to matters of men, refused to let her move or be scared of Green.

"You're not human, are you?"

"No," he bit out, keeping his eyes closed.

"I'm not human either, Green."

"I know." He still refused to meet her gaze.

"Yet, you want me to leave you alone because you think I don't want you or that I'll be scared of you?"

His jaw lined tightened. "That and if I do take you, Melanie, it will mean you're my wife. You don't want marriage. You don't want a man like me for eternity. You have no desire to spend your life with any one man, let alone me."

Everything he said was true or at least she thought it had been. It didn't feel true anymore. The idea of knowing he'd always be there didn't scare her as it should. It comforted her.

This is a man I could love.

Shocked by her own thoughts, Melanie went to scramble off Green's lap. He caught her waist and held her in place. "I'm sorry, baby. I am. This isn't how I wanted you to find out what I am. I'll call Wilson to come and get you. I'll--"

Outraged that he'd try to push her off on another man, Melanie slapped him hard in the face. His eyes snapped open and she glared at him. "Thaddeus Chandler Green, I am not scared of you. I'm scared of how I feel for you. I just met you. I shouldn't want to spend the rest of however long of a life I have with you. And how dare you try to hand me over to Wilson?"

His brows rose. "You want to spend the rest of your life with me? I'm boring. I'm not like the men you date. I don't run around kicking in doors and getting so shit faced I can hardly stand."

Melanie snorted. "No, you just run around punching men non-stop. Big difference. Gawd, for a genius, you are really lacking in the intelligence department at the moment. Really. You are. Why would you ever want anything to do with me beyond sex? I have nothing to offer anyone, especially not a man like you. You're amazing. I can't hold a candle to you, Thad."

He slid one arm around her waist and lifted her a bit. She thought he was going to move her off his lap. When she felt the head of his cock pressing against her wet core, she knew differently.

His eyes locked with hers. "If we do this, I won't be able to be gentle the first time and there is a better than average chance I'll partially shift. I'll sink my teeth into you and fill you so full of my cum that you're head might spin." He drew in a ragged breath. "This is your chance to walk away. There is no going back. Once I claim you, you are my mate, my wife, until the end of our days, Melanie. Do you still want me?"

"Yes," she whispered, leaning in to kiss him. The second she pressed her mouth to his, Green slid his tongue in. Fire exploded throughout her body and she ate at his mouth, hungry for even more. His cock mirrored his tongue, thrusting into her body with a force that made her yelp into his mouth. His girth left Melanie feeling as if Green might actually tear her up the center. She cried out as the pain from having something the size of his cock in her moved through her. What felt like an eternity for her body to adjust to his cock was merely seconds.

Letting out a long breath, Melanie tipped her head back. "Oh, gawd, Thad."

Green growled and nipped playfully at her neck. "You're so tight."

A slow, sexy smile covered her mouth as he kissed to her lips. It always amazed men just how tight she was. It came from the blood of the nymphs that coursed through her veins. The minute she was settled over his massive cock, Green held her hips firmly, not allowing her any movement.

She met his gaze and found his emerald green eyes swirling. His breathing was irregular and his jaw set. Leaning forward, she pressed her lips to his and released her power, letting it coat him and hopefully giving him some much needed control over the beast he was fighting.

Green's eyes widened as he returned her kiss. She laced her tongue around his and began to ride him, slow at first, doing her best to get used to his size. He growled as he thrust his hips up and fucked her hard, fast and furious. He filled her so completely that Melanie could barely form a thought above how good it felt. The next thing she knew, Green had her pressed against the keyboard as he knocked the piano bench away and rose to his feet, never once exiting her body. He pumped harder, thrusting her into the piano. Random notes played as she clung to him, desperate to accept all he offered.

"Mine," he ground out, moving his aggressive kisses to her neck.

He made her so wet, so hot for him that Melanie couldn't recall a time she'd ever been this close to coming so soon after a man entered her body. Everything about him excited her. His smell. His hard body. His long, thick cock. She couldn't get enough.

"Mine." Green yanked on her hips, driving her body onto his with such a force she could scarcely remember to breathe. The sounds of sex sounded around her. Not only could she feel their powerful joining, she could hear the wet slickness of their bodies as they became one. So much pleasure. So much power. She never wanted it to end.

"Tell me," he gritted his teeth, "that you're mine, Melanie." Green took her body with a force she never in a million years expected him to do. What should have been too painful for her to enjoy, was anything but. It was exactly what she needed. He was exactly what she needed.

She melted beneath him. Seeing Green's dominant side shine through made Melanie want to submit fully and forever. It was something she never did. Yet she surrendered to it. "Yes, yours, Thad. Always yours."

Pleasure built, deep within her abdomen and Melanie knew she was close to coming. Green fucked her with the fierceness of a possessed man and she loved every second of it. His passion was raw. There were no guards, no defenses, no books to hide behind. Just Thad.

Green pummeled her body with his. Taking hold of the sides of his face, Melanie brought his lips to hers and kissed him passionately. His tongue stroked her mouth to ecstasy, doing little to stop her pending orgasm. Her power continued to run over him, hopefully giving him the edge he needed to stay in control of his beast. She wasn't afraid of him or what he carried but Melanie didn't want to share Green with the beast, at least not yet. She just wanted him.

He felt so good, so right inside her that Melanie couldn't hide her moans. The minute they escaped, Green let out an animalistic growl and took her with so much strength she wasn't sure how she didn't break. The strangest thing of all was that Melanie wanted even more. "Harder," she panted.

Green obliged. Her orgasm tore through her with an intensity she'd never felt before. Never had it felt this good to be with a man, this right. Her pussy began to spasm uncontrollably, clenching down on Green's cock. Slamming into her, he went to the hilt and stilled. An explosion of hot warmth filled her and she knew then he was coming as well. Having never allowed a man to release his cum in her, Melanie was a bit shocked at how much Green seemed to have and how very warm it was.

* * * *

Green stayed rooted in Melanie, continuing to fill her with his seed. It was surreal. He'd thought for sure he'd lose control and bite her. He didn't and he knew why. Melanie had helped him control the beast with her magik so the man could be with her. "Thank you."

A sultry laugh came from her as she clung to him. "No, thank you."

The woman was too much. Too perfect. He caressed her gently, staying deep within her and knew he'd filled her so full of cum that their combined juices were now seeping from their joined bodies. She wiggled a bit and his cock came to life, hardening instantly.

A slow smile curved over her lips. "*Mmm*, insatiable. I like that in a man."

"Are you sore?" he asked, knowing he was rougher than he'd wanted to be with her. In truth, he'd been rougher than he'd ever been with Elizabeth.

A pang of guilt tore through him. Elizabeth had been the woman he'd pledged his life to yet he'd never felt like this with her. Yet here she was, back as part of Melanie. Had he not witnessed the marvel of it all, Green wouldn't have believed they were really the same person. A piece of him was ashamed of how intense his feelings for Melanie were. If he didn't know better, he'd say he loved her more than he'd ever loved Elizabeth. That couldn't be right. He'd only just met Melanie and even though she was his wife reincarnated, he'd seen enough to know she wasn't "his" Elizabeth.

Melanie purred ever so softly. "I'm a little sore, but I want more." Her brow creased and he could sense a question waiting to come out.

Leaning forward, Green captured a nipple in his mouth and sucked gently before letting it go. "Tell me what's wrong. Do you regret it?"

"No," she said and he knew she was telling the truth. "I just never thought I'd get married let alone do it in a rather unconventional way."

It took everything in Green not to tell Melanie that they were not husband and wife yet. He had to bite her, claim her fully for them to be a mated pair. Her magik had aided in keeping the beast within him at bay so it could be just the two of them.

She ran her hands through his hair. "Tell me that you don't regret it, Green. Your eyes look troubled."

"I'm a little surprised you're taking being my wife so well," he said, wanting to test the water with Melanie. Not only that, but his unease about Elizabeth and feelings of betrayal were fast becoming almost impossible to bear.

Her cheeks flared pink as she glanced away. "Umm, Thad?"

"Yes."

"Would you be willing to marry me in a church so my family can be there? My Dad's a diehard fan of handfasting if you prefer that but I'd like them to be able to be part of it somehow. I think my father gave up hope I'd ever settle down. I'd like to do it soon, if you don't mind."

His chest tightened. "You want to say vows in front of friends and family?"

Melanie nodded and his heart soared. She wanted him and wanted others to know it. He kissed her lips and began to slide in and out of her slowly. "Yes, honey. We can do that. We can do anything you want."

"Anything?" She gave him a wanton smile as he rode her body.

Melanie felt so good. So perfect that Green could barely think beyond the moment. Her slit quivered around his cock, grasping at him, doing its best to pull him back into her warmth. Reaching between their bodies, Green rubbed her clit.

"Ah, yes," she panted.

Thrusting into her, Green knew he'd never get enough. Melanie was like a drug. One he hoped to never kick. He lifted her, allowing her to wrap her long legs around his waist, and moved. It didn't matter where he carried her only that he moved. Too much energy was building around him. Melanie's power was overwhelming and the beast within while stunned into slight submission had been with him too long to completely deny. The next thing Green knew, he had Melanie pressed to the wall and was drilling his cock into her, eliciting gasps and tiny cries from her. She dug her fingernails into the backs of his arms and the second he smelled blood, he lost what little control he had. He slammed into Melanie's body so hard that a painting fell to the floor, taking with it a vase from the table beneath it. Still, he didn't stop. He couldn't.

"Too ... too ... much," Melanie said, her voice barely there between her moans.

"Not," he thrust into her again, "nearly," grabbing her hands, he pinned them to the wall, "fucking enough."

A slow, sexy smile curved over her sweet lips as she countered his movements, taking him even deeper. Green couldn't have stopped himself even if he wanted to. He was too far gone. It had been too long since he'd know the pleasures of a woman and even then, none compared to Melanie. Not even Elizabeth.

Desperate to rid his mind of Elizabeth, Green drew on his beast's strength. He fucked Melanie harder, staying just this side of hurting her. A spasm tore through her pussy as her orgasm struck. He was powerless to stop his own. Ramming into her, he exploded, filling her with his cum. "Ah, fuck, yeah. Take it. Take all of it."

His words sounded foreign to him. Never before had he outwardly expressed so much raw emotion. Melanie brought out a carnal side of him that Green wasn't sure he liked.

She went limp against him and he could sense the toll he'd taken on her already weakened body. Kissing his neck softly, Melanie laid her head against his chest. Every part of Green knew she needed to rest, needed to regain what little strength she had but he couldn't help himself. His cock hardened almost instantly.

"You want more?" she asked, not bothering to lift her head.

He knew he shouldn't want anymore from her--that his first concern should be her safety and well being--but that wasn't what happened. He nodded. "I want more."

"I'm tired. Can we rest just a little?"

Green wanted to tell her that was fine. He couldn't. He needed more. The only answer he gave was in the form of his hips moving as he began fucking her again. Melanie kissed his neck softly, never once complaining that he needed more from her. He only hoped he'd be able to get his fill soon. For both their sakes.

Chapter Ten

"Are you okay?" Peren asked, a smile graced her face. Her green eyes held something else, perhaps concern. It was no surprise to Melanie. Peren wasn't one for dropping bombshells on others and this was certainly one. For the past few hours, Melanie had listened as Peren and Missy attempted to bring her up to speed. All they'd succeeded in doing was confusing her more. All the talk of immortal operatives, the Paranormal Security and Intelligence Agency and friends she'd known all her life being anything but human had her normally capable mind dizzy. So many signs had been given to her over her twenty-plus years yet she'd missed them all. Melanie had seen only what she wanted to see and nothing more.

Wilson chuckled. His chocolate-brown eyes held no mockery, only genuine compassion and she appreciated that more than he'd ever know. It was easy to see he enjoyed being the butt of every joke, the group comedian but Wilson had a heart of gold. "I'm guessing by the blank look on her face that Melanie is anything but fine."

Melanie pointed at Wilson as she sat across the table from the majority of the members of the I-Ops team. Lukian and Green were piloting the private jet. Roi had offered to sit in for Green but there had been a unanimous "no" from the rest of the men. Lukian had muttered something about a fence and how he didn't want to see if Roi could go off road with the jet but Melanie didn't question it. "Let me see if I've got this straight. You're a rat?"

"No," Wilson bit out. "I'm a man who can shift into a rat. And other weird stuff lately." He squirmed as his gaze raced around the area. "Stuff I'm not talking about."

Other stuff? As much as she wanted to question him, she didn't.

"A man who can shift into a rat?" Roi whistled. "*Big difference.* Yeah, thanks for clearing that up for all of us. I'd ask what the other stuff is but I've got a pretty good idea." He rubbed his stubble-covered chin. "You know, they make creams for that now."

"Fuck off," Wilson said.

Melanie looked at Roi. "And you're a wolf?"

He grinned and Melanie watched in horror as his teeth lengthened. Missy slapped him and Roi pulled her onto his lap. "What? How could I resist the chance to do that?"

"Easy, act somewhere close to your age," Missy said, arching a brow playfully.

Eadan snorted. "Wouldn't he need a cane or something then?"

Ignoring her brother's comment, Melanie glanced at Jon. He'd been quiet for the most part, seeming to soak in her response to them all. His blond hair was cut much closer than any of the other I-Ops'. Jon screamed good ol' boy. That all-American guy everyone loves. Something told Melanie he was more than he appeared to be, not just talking form shifting either. "And you're a tiger ... err ... able to shift into a tiger?"

"Yes ma'am. I can and am." His voice was tinged with the South. She couldn't help but smile at how polite he was. Whatever he kept hidden from the rest of the I-Ops wasn't evil. That much she knew. It was just extremely personal to Jon and dark. She couldn't help but like him. Hell, she liked them all, even Wilson. No--especially Wilson.

Peren smiled and lifted her brows. "You're not freaking out. I'm impressed."

Melanie shrugged. In truth, she'd been petrified that her friends wouldn't accept her if they knew she was Fae. Never did she suspect they were different, too. She also never knew that Missy and Eadan had been married for several years or that they'd lost a child. Her gaze went from Missy to Eadan and tears filled her eyes. The ordeal had to have been horrific and she should have been there to comfort them both. Feeling someone watching her closely, Melanie looked up to find Roi staring at her. She did her best to blink away the tears but one still managed to escape. "Sorry."

Roi shook his head. "Don't be. I would never ask Missy to forget her time with your brother."

"It's just that I never knew I was almost an aunt or that Missy was my sister-in-law. I'd have liked to know that. I wouldn't have told anyone." Melanie glanced at her brother. "And I would have liked to have been there for you, Eadan, to help you through it all."

Eadan took her hand in his and nodded, keeping his lips pressed tight. It was clear it still hurt him and it broke Melanie's heart to see him that way. He'd always been so strong and yet so full of humor. Letting her magik up, she pushed it over him, easing his pain. He cocked his head as his forehead creased.

"Mel, what did you just do?"

"Eased your pain as much as I could and...." She stopped, not wanting to confess all of what she'd just done.

"And what?" Missy asked. She reached for Eadan but stopped just short of touching him.

"And I sort of cleared Eadan's pain to the point he will look for his true mate soon. I want him to be happy, Missy. You have Roi and little ones on the way. I want Eadan to not only find his mate but seize the moment without regret."

Missy slid off Roi's lap, leaned over Eadan and hugged Melanie. "I want him happy too, Melanie. He will always be one of my best friends. Wait a minute. Did you say little ones--as in plural?"

Melanie nodded in affirmation. "Yes. Why?"

"I'm having twins?"

Unsure how to answer that, she glanced at Peren since she'd always been the one who seemed to act as the glue within their friendship. It was Peren who Missy and Melanie went to whenever they felt as though their lives were falling apart. It was she who managed to bring them together. The three had always been inseparable. The last three weeks had pulled at that bond but not broken it. "Umm?"

Peren grinned from ear to ear. "Tell me that she's having twins because I cannot wait for Roi to be peed on by more than one baby."

"Well, they won't have very good aim since they're girls but I think they will give their father a run for his money," Melanie said, chancing a glance at Roi.

"Girls?" Roi's face paled. He clutched the edge of the table with one hand and pulled Missy to him tighter with the other. "Two?"

Missy squealed as she hugged him around the neck. Another noise came from her and for a moment, Melanie thought for sure Missy would choke the life from Roi. Apparently, Eadan thought so as well.

"Missy-bean, try not to kill your husband. You're newlyweds."

She giggled as she pressed her lips to Roi's scruffy cheek. "Ohmygods, Roi. We're having more than one baby!"

"Two girls?"

Melanie nodded.

Roi gulped so loud Melanie heard it from across the table. "If they are anything like their mother, I am so screwed." He looked like he was about to be sick. "They are never allowed to date! Ever! And if one of them brings home a supernatural guy, I'm gutting him. I'll not have any man with the stamina of our kind...." He rubbed his eyes. "Aww, no man can touch them. Supernatural or not."

Wilson laughed as he ran a hand through his shagged chestnut hair. "Mmm, lesbian action is good, too."

Jon sighed as Eadan thrust power at Wilson, knocking him back in his seat a bit. "No one is touching my goddaughters! Man or woman!"

Nodding, Roi patted Eadan's shoulder. "We should work on our intimidation techniques."

Melanie shook her head. "No. You're good. Trust me on this. Men will run, shaking from the room the minute their eyes land on the likes of you guys. Just promise not to shoot anyone before they at least get their name out."

Roi's nostril's flared. "You want me to waste bullets on randy punks who only have one thing on their minds? No. Not good enough."

Arching a brow, Missy laughed. "It's a damn good thing my father didn't share your opinion or you'd be dead." She flicked his chin lightly with her first finger. "Need I remind you how very 'randy' you are?"

Wilson and Jon made gagging noises.

Everyone laughed, making the tension in Melanie ebb away. It was quickly replaced by fatigue. Glancing at her brother, she let him sense how physically exhausted she was. As a fellow Fae he would be able to detect how sick she truly was. When Missy, Peren and Wilson gasped she realized she's messed up and sent the signal out to too many people.

Wilson was next to her before she could blink. He eased her to her feet gently. "Come on, Mels. There are beds in the back portion of the jet. You can sleep for awhile."

She hesitated. "Umm, I don't want to be alone right now, Wilson. I was planning to beg Eadan to sit with me. I get the sense he's the only male Green won't punch if found near me while I was alone in a room--on a bed for that matter. I kind of like you, even with the rat thing, and don't want to see Green kill you."

Peren and Missy laughed as they made their way to her. Peren slid her arm around Melanie's waist. "Sweetie, we're pregnant and tired. How about we rest with you. The beds are big enough to fit all three of us. How's that?"

"I *so* want to watch that," Wilson said with a wink.

"I don't like the idea of stealing Green's kill, but I'll do it." Roi cracked his knuckles. "The lesbian comment is still lingering in the back of my mind. Killing you might put that at ease." He lifted his arms. "Not that I'm saying my girls can't live the life they want. I just don't want Wilson thinking he's getting any ... aww ... I can't even say it. That's it. You die."

Eadan shook his head and white-blond wisps of his hair broke free from the tie that held them back. "I'm going to have to put a protective bubble of power over Wilson before the week's out. Poor guy. I'd give ya a lucky rabbit's foot or something but I'm starting to think you'd need the whole damn rabbit."

* * * *

Melanie let the girls lead her back to a room with an oversized white bed in it. She climbed in gingerly, doing her best not to wince as pain shot through her lower back. Peren and Missy sandwiched her, hugging her close. They were her best friends, sisters of the heart even and she would miss them horribly when she was gone. She'd miss all of the I-Ops and her family as well. The thought of leaving Green made a sob tear free from her.

"Mel?" Peren asked, hugging her tighter.

"How long did you know Lukian before you knew you loved him?"

Peren let out a soft, soothing laugh. "I think it was instantaneous."

Missy grumbled. "I couldn't stand my husband when I first met him. He grew quickly on me though. How long before you knew you loved Green?"

Love Green?

Melanie almost denied the claim but couldn't. She chose to avoid giving an answer. "I married him ... err ... I mean mated with him, I guess they call it that."

The sound that came from Missy made Melanie jump. Missy grabbed her arm. "Ohmygods, why didn't you tell us the minute you boarded? Hell, the minute you spotted us?"

Melanie averted her gaze. "Because I don't think he's very happy about it. I referred to him as my husband a couple of times and this weird look came over his face. I'd say it was one of regret. That's the best way I can describe it."

"Do you love him, Melanie?" Peren asked, something in the tone of her voice was different.

"I think so. I'm not exactly sure what love is, Peren, but I know that I was fine with the idea of dying before Green came into my life. The thought of being away from him terrifies me. The thought of him being harmed on account of me scares me even more. I want to wrap my arms around him and will us somewhere that he'll always be safe. Somewhere we can always be together."

"Have you told him that you love him?"

"No, but he's never told me that he loves me either so I'm guessing he doesn't. It makes sense. We've not known each other very long."

Peren grunted as she rolled out of the bed. "I'll be right back. Get some rest."

"Peren?"

She didn't stop.

* * * *

"I never pegged you for a fucking idiot, Green," Peren said, coming through the cockpit doorway with the look of a crazed woman. Her auburn hair hung in waves over her shoulders and the fire in her eyes told Green he was in trouble though he was unsure as to why.

Green glanced at Lukian. "Care to shed some light as to why your mate looks like she wants to slit my throat?"

Lukian shrugged. He had a way about him that rarely was riled. On the night Lukian had met Peren, he'd let that mask fall. He'd shown his fear for her safety and his hatred of the men trying to harm her. It was that moment that alerted Green that Lukian had found his true mate. "I do my best to avoid speaking for her. She scares me when she's pissed."

"Yes, you *scream* alpha male," Green mused, unable to stop the twitch of his lips as he fought back a smile. Lukian prided himself on his ability to rule. After all, the man was the king of the lycans. Royal and powerful but wherever Peren was concerned, he was powerless to her desires. It was love in its rawest form.

Peren pushed Green's shoulder not letting up on her seemingly unprovoked assault. "How stupid are you? Seriously."

"Umm?" He wasn't sure how to answer that since technically he was a genius. Off the charts in fact. Green thought it best to remain silent and allow the obviously hormonal woman to have her say.

Laughing, Lukian stared at his wife. "Baby, you're going to need to spell out whatever is bothering you. Green's a man, not a mind reader. We tend to miss hints women give us."

She snorted. "No shit! Really?"

Green swallowed hard. "I'm sensing some sarcasm. Everything okay?"

"No, everything is not okay! One of my best friends is lying in your room, riddled with pain and convinced she's married to a man who doesn't love her."

"You mated with Melanie?" Lukian asked, shock evident in his voice. "I didn't smell your mark on her."

"He didn't mate with her." Peren pushed Green again. "But he let Melanie think he did. That girl has never loved a man outside of her brother and father, yet she just admitted to being in love with you. How dare you lie to her? How dare you hurt her, Green? She's dying. Why in the hell would let her think you were her husband if you don't care for her--if you don't love her?"

"Peren, baby, it's not our business." Lukian's tone was stern, though the way he squared his shoulders told Green he was as pissed at him as Peren was. Maybe more so.

Peren didn't seem to notice or care for Lukian's display of dominance. "Melanie is more worried about dying and leaving you alone than she is of actually dying, Green. How could you lie to her? How could you let her believe you're her husband when you're not?"

"You lied to me?"

The sound of Melanie's voice made his chest tightened. He didn't turn around, he couldn't. "Answer me, Thad, did you lie to me about the two of us being married or mated, whatever you call it?"

"Did he bite you when he was fucking you?" Peren asked, her tone sharp. Tension filled the small cabin to the point Green almost choked on it.

He wanted to shout out that he didn't "fuck" Melanie, that he made love to her but Peren was right. He had fucked her. It had been raw, carnal and nothing like what he should have given to her. Nothing like what she deserved.

"I'll take your silence as a yes." The pain in Melanie's voice nearly did him in. He could take Peren and Lukian's disapproval but hers would be the death of him. Yet still he said nothing in defense of himself. It wasn't a matter for all to hear and it wasn't as if he had a reason for lying or rather, omitting the truth in regards to being mated to her. "She warned me but I didn't listen. I should have listened."

"Who warned you about what?" Missy asked, pushing her way into the suddenly cramped cockpit.

Wonderful, one more of them to assemble on the other side.

"Elizabeth told me to stay away from him. She knew he'd do this to me."

Green knew Melanie was crying. He could hear it in her voice but he didn't turn to look at her. He couldn't. Seeing her upset and knowing he caused it would be his undoing. It wasn't as if he could whisk her away to somewhere they could be alone. Somewhere he could make love to her as he should have and lay claim to her.

Peren smacked him once more. "Asshole!"

"Leave him alone," Melanie whispered, pain evident in her sweet voice. "I'm tired and every muscle in my body is sore. Missy, will you ask Eadan if I can stay with him once we land?"

"Sure, sweetie."

"You can bunk with me if you want," Wilson said softly, appearing behind Melanie. "I won't try anything, Mels. You have my word. Consider it a semi-asshole free zone."

Every ounce of Green wanted to attack Wilson. How dare he try to get Melanie into his bed? How dare he blatantly come onto his wife?

My wife? She's not my wife and that's what got me into this mess to begin with.

He drew in a deep, ragged breath, waiting to hear Melanie dismiss Wilson's offer. When she didn't, he spun in his seat to look at her, only to find Wilson guiding her toward the back of the jet--straight to his room. The beast within Green surged, nearly breaking free.

It was Peren who controlled it. Green would never harm a woman, beast form or not, and Peren knew it. She glared at him. "You don't deserve her and you have no say with what she does with what's left of her life!"

Peren stormed off, leaving Green to dwell on the truths she'd spewed forth. He shifted a bit before double checking the gauges. Lukian cleared his throat. "She's right, you know?"

"I know." Green nodded.

"Doll baby, you cannot throw Green from the plane!" Roi shouted.

Green and Lukian glanced back to see Missy and Peren doing their best to get past Jon and Roi. When Green spotted a parachute in Missy's hands, he glanced at Lukian. "Tell me you aren't going to let them toss me out."

"They're pregnant and pissed." Lukian gave him a once over. "You're part cat. You'll land on your feet, right?"

"Not from this altitude!" He wasn't sure if Lukian was serious or not. Prior to Lukian mating with Peren, Green wouldn't have ever thought his long-time friend would allow him to be pushed from anything. Being mated certainly changed Lukian. In the span of three weeks, the lycan King had done a complete turnaround. He'd do just about anything to see his wife happy and that meant assuring her friend was cared for.

"Well, they do have a parachute, so I'll think you'll live," Lukian said, peering down the end of his nose. His blue eyes locked on Green. "Besides, I sort of hope I'm the one who gets to push you." He motioned towards the back of the jet and grinned.

Green followed his gaze. "Gee, thanks."

"Anytime."

Jon put his hand out and caught Peren a second before she would have made it past him. The fact Peren didn't level Jon spoke volumes as to how much she respected him. He appeared appreciative. "Sorry, ma'am, but I can't let you toss him out. His skills come in handy. Toss Wilson. I can't think of anything he has to offer that we really need."

"Ooo," Roi nodded eagerly, "that's a great idea. The two of you can push Wilson out. You don't even need the parachute. Here give me that thing. No sense wasting resources. The government will just love us if we show them we're making cutbacks."

Jon laughed. "Yeah, consider pushing Wilson to his death cutbacks."

"I heard that!" Wilson yelled from the back of the jet.

Eadan chuckled as he leaned against the back wall. The minute his eyes fell on Green, the smile faded from his face. Green couldn't really blame the guy for being pissed. Melanie was his sister. He wanted the best for her. Green did too.

Standing, Green stared down at Lukian. "I'll be right back."

"I advise against going anywhere near those two at the moment. They're likely to really do it. And if you insist on doing it, keep in mind that unless you lose your head or pierce your heart," he clucked his tongue on his cheek, "you'll most likely survive. It won't be pretty but you'll live."

"Oh, you're real funny. I'm dying here. Really."

"I do try."

Ignoring Lukian, Green headed for Wilson's room. Peren and Missy shared "kill him" looks as he neared them. He put his hands up, signaling surrender. "I wanted to claim her. The beast wanted to as well. She used her power to help me control it. I thought she understood that I had to bite her. When she commented on being married, I was too stunned to hear she was happy to tell her the truth."

"Do you love her?" Peren asked, cutting to the chase.

"That's between Melanie and me. Once we figure everything out, we'll be sure to let you all know," he said sardonically. He went to move but found himself held in place by an unseen force. Instantly, his gaze went to Eadan. "Let go of me."

"She's resting. Something about Wilson calms her. The minute he wrapped his arms around her, I felt her system stop its inner struggle. Let her sleep."

Green's jaw tightened and his fists clenched as he glared at Eadan. "He better not be touching my wife!"

Tipping his head, Eadan's lip curled. "Herein lies the problem. She is not your wife, Green. Not this time around."

Shocked, Green took a step back.

Eadan cast a smug look in his direction. "Dad filled me in on all I needed to know prior to coming. I'm up to speed on the situation. As are the rest of the Ops."

This was more than he was willing to deal with at the moment. He needed to get to Melanie to straighten things out between them. He didn't need to stand and be judged by people who didn't fully understand what was going on. "Let me through."

"No." Eadan splayed his hands and quirked an eyebrow, as if daring Green to try to go through him.

For a split second, Green entertained the idea. Knowing it would upset Melanie more, if in the end, her brother was harmed, he reined his temper as best he could. Eadan leaned against the seat next to him and crossed one foot over the other, looking entirely too cocky for Green's liking.

"Give her time, Green."

"She doesn't have time," he whispered, knowing each moment with her was precious.

Eadan nodded. "I know."

* * * *

Roi cornered his mate near the back of the jet, snaking his arm around her waist and pulling her against his chest. He growled as he took in her sweet scent, now combined with his since she carried his children within her. "Mmm, twins."

Missy laughed, rubbing against him. "Are you going to be okay? You passed out cold when you found out you were going to be a daddy. I'd like a 'heads up' if I should alert the others."

"Ha, ha," he said, bending and pressing his lips to her temple. "I love you."

"I love you too but I'd love you more if you'd let Peren and me push Green from the jet," she said, her voice sugar sweet.

"Missy doll, I told you I was fine with Wilson going." He wagged his brows as he nipped playfully at her ear.

She purred--a trait she had due to the excessive amount of various strands of cat DNA she carried with in. The sound drove Roi mad with need. "Mmm, baby, do that again and I'll be buried in you before we land."

Missy turned in his arms and leveled a serious stare on him. "Promise me that you won't let Green--"

Knowing he couldn't make promises involving someone else's life, Roi silenced her with a kiss. When he pulled back, he expected Missy to ask again. She didn't. Instead, she put her head against his chest and sighed. Her fingers caressed his sides gently. "I want them to be as happy as we are."

"I know," he whispered, holding her to him.

"I want Eadan happy, too, Roi."

"I know, Missy doll. I know."

Chapter Eleven

One Week Later…

Green moved slowly, leading Wilson and Jon along the edge of the river. The oxygen-rich Amazon was humid and seemed to be an entity all its own. Green and Jon were the only two team members who hadn't spent the morning complaining about the heat. Even under the canopy of the jungle's trees, it was warm. Jon originated from the south and seemed to relish the heat. Wilson, on the other hand, hated it.

Glancing over his shoulder, he caught sight of Wilson smacking the back of his neck and cursing under his breath about the mosquitoes seeming to like the taste of him more than anyone else. Green caught Jon snickering. Something moved in the distance and Green tossed a closed fist up as he dropped to one knee. Wilson and Jon followed suit. They were miles from their base camp on a reconnaissance mission.

Pointing at Jon, Green motioned for him to ensure that they weren't being flanked. Amber eyes stared out from Jon's cammed up face. The bushrag head and torso ghillie he had on made him look like a moving compost pile, not a man, just as it was designed to do. The suit covered the outline of his body and weapon so he blended with his surroundings. The rest of the team went with tactical vest and camouflage fatigues. The foliage on the rainforest floor wasn't as dense as most people assumed it would be. The canopy above acts as a light filter and also reduces the amount of rain that actually hits the ground. So, while certain portions are so thick it's difficult to see your hand before your face, others are thin enough to move through with ease. The suits did aid in blending into spots that were covered in brush. It also gave them peace of mind.

Green twisted a bit and bumped a woody vine. A small shadow moved overhead and Green's gaze locked on it. The second he found a tiny brown monkey staring down at him with a curious expression, he decided against attacking. His luck, the monkey would end up being a byproduct from Krauss' experiments and decapitate him while he wasn't looking.

Green shook the thought from his head.

Wilson visually scanned the area, clutching his M60 close. Green couldn't help but think of Missy's comment when she'd put the order in for weapons. The minute she'd mentioned Wilson must be compensating for something, the entire team had lost it, laughing to the point they were snorting.

Green was comfortable with his M16 and a Desert Eagle sidearm. If worse came to worse, he could shift into a panther and tear someone's head clean off. Of course, with Krauss' experiments the likelihood of his enemy possessing similar if not better skills was great. They'd no doubt posses the ability to regenerate severed heads. That or they'd sic the monkey on him.

Always comforting.

He glanced up to find it grinning at him like it understood his line of thinking.

"Bravo Dog One, we've tagged the area in question and are heading to rendezvous point." Lukian's voice filtered through Green's earpiece. Reaching up, he clicked his com three times to indicate he heard but could not respond.

"Enemy?" Lukian asked.

Green didn't respond.

"Unknown?"

He clicked twice more to indicate yes. Sniffing the air, he let his supernatural senses take the lead. Aside from the normal smells of the jungle, Green couldn't pick up on anything different. Still, he knew he heard something. Since the monkey hadn't moved, he ruled it out. Now, as for any of the monkey's little buddies showing up, that was a different matter.

"What the fuck?" Wilson called out, a second before he fired a small burst. Birds scattered and the jungle seemed to flare to life.

Green turned to see what it was Wilson was firing at and found a man with some sort of blow dart weapon about a foot from him. Since it was unheard of for anyone to be able to sneak up on him, he was shocked. "Don't shoot!"

Seeing the blank look on the man's face, Green quickly repeated what he'd said in several regional dialects, hoping one would be the man's.

"That little bastard over there shot me with an arrow!" Wilson yelled. The low rumble that emanated from his throat told Green his friend was on the verge of a shift. Once he did that, killing would be inevitable.

Green ducked and spun around the native tribesman with the blow dart. Each man there barely came to mid-chest level on him and looked to have placed a bowl over their head and cut their hair. The tribesman whispered something that Green surmised to be "man demon." In his culture that was exactly what the I-Ops were.

He spoke quickly, mixing dialects from the region, hoping to get one right. When the native bowed his head and put his hands in the air, Green exhaled.

Jon stood at his full height and the natives lifted their crude but effective weapons once more. "Green, what did I do?"

"You look like a walking and talking tree to them, Jon," Green said, suppressing a laugh. Now was not the time for jokes but he had to admit, it was funny. "Shift into a tiger, they're sure to think you're a god as well."

"They think we're gods?"

Green listened as the natives spoke amongst themselves, lowering their weapons once more. "In a way. They believed us to be man demons at first."

"What did you tell them to make them think otherwise?" Jon asked.

Green scratched his chin. "To be honest, I've no idea. I thought it was along the lines of we come in peace. Then he bowed and I'm not so sure."

Wilson hissed. "Where's a fucking pen when I need one? Science Geek admitted to not knowing the answer to something."

Ignoring Wilson, Green watched the natives converse among themselves. They pointed toward the sky and then back at the I-Ops before one jabbed another in the chest. They formed a line and then disappeared as quickly as they'd come, leaving Wilson holding his upper thigh, Jon slinking back toward them and Green stupefied.

"Bravo Team?"

Touching his com unit, Green sighed. "We're fine. Well," he glanced at Wilson, "alive. Though, the natives are truly restless."

Wilson nudged him. "Tell him they're most likely preparing a bonfire to roast us with now too. Bastards." He clutched his leg and growled.

Green eased Wilson's arm over his shoulder, taking the majority of the man's weight off his bad leg. "Nah, I don't think rats are high on their food chain either. You're good."

Jon snickered and Wilson groaned. "Sure, now Green develops a sense of humor."

* * * *

"Fuck you," Wilson bit out as Green tried to inspect the wound on his upper right thigh. "I don't want you touching me."

"I believe the arrow you were hit with was poisoned. It would be in your best interest to allow me to clean it and verify whether or not poison is involved." Green attempted again to get a better look at it but Wilson wasn't having anything to do with it. Other than Jon, none of the men were being particular friendly to him. Even Jon was reserved, more so than normal.

Setting his medical bag aside, Green rubbed his temples. It had all gone too far. For the past week, he'd watched as his friends, men he considered brothers pull away from him, eschewing him for something he didn't intentionally do. It wasn't as if he set out to hurt Melanie. Hell, he'd been ecstatic the minute she acknowledged she was not only happy being his wife but wanted to recite their vows in front of family and friends.

How did I let it get this out of control?

"Since you're being a pigheaded jerk, will you at least let me take a look at it?" Melanie asked, catching Green off guard.

He jerked back, letting her through. Her smell, lavender and lilac, drove him mad and the urge to pull her into his arms was great. The thin, white blouse she had on left her nipples showing through and it was all he could do to keep his hands to himself. He knew the sweetness of having her berry-like nubs in his mouth. He knew the look upon her face when her orgasm struck and the feel of her pussy as it clenched around his cock. He wanted it all again. He wanted it for always--he wanted her.

Brushing past him, Melanie made his entire body burn with need. He'd spent every night since they'd landed, watching over her, sleeping by her side without her knowing. Green would leave her room just before she woke, allowing her to believe that he'd given her the space she'd needed. It was lie. Eadan was aware of his deception because Green switched rooms with him so he could be alone with Melanie.

She seemed to have gotten a bit more energy over the last week. Green's only guess was that it had something to due with the fact she was actually sleeping through the night now. Eadan had been shocked but he seemed to think she rested soundly because Green was near, holding her as she slept. Since Melanie refused to submit to any testing or even speak with him in daylight hours, Green wasn't sure what was happening. He only hoped the end results left her alive and well. There was no way he could or would live without her. She just didn't know it yet.

Melanie bent down in front of Wilson. "You've got two choices. You can either take your pants down or I can cut up the leg to get a better look at this."

Every one of the Ops present made a noise indicating she'd astonished them all. Eadan was the one who voiced their concern. Since he was a blood relative, it seemed like the best choice. Melanie had proven she could take out a small army by standing in one spot and Green didn't want to test her patience.

Eadan on the other hand didn't seem too worried about his sister snapping and removing any vital body parts. "Mel, what the hell are you going to do? Shop the wound away? Last time I checked, we hadn't put Wilson on sale or offered a certain percentage off him so could you please go back to wandering around, picking pretty flowers and 'oooing' shiny things?"

Everyone but Eadan leaned back. Even Wilson looked a little suspicious as to whether or not Melanie would blow.

To Green's surprise, Melanie ignored Eadan and opened Green's bag of medical supplies. She pulled a bottle of distilled water from it. "Pants down. Now."

Wilson mumbled something that Green's supernatural hearing couldn't even pick up. Sliding back a bit, Wilson tried and failed to get away.

"What?" Melanie asked, not letting up at all.

He sighed. "I said that I'm not wearing any underwear."

"I've seen many cocks, Wilson. Unless you've sprouted a third testicle or a second shaft, I think I'm good."

Green growled. The thought of Melanie being anywhere near Wilson's dick was too much for him. It didn't help that he knew she had indeed seen a good many cocks. His would be the only one she's ever see again. She was his mate, his wife.

No. Not my wife yet. But she will be.

Jon laid a hand on Green's shoulder, calming him slightly. "Easy. Attacking him won't fix anything."

Melanie grabbed a pair of scissors from the bag and cut Wilson's pant leg open. She hissed when she saw the wound. It was a nasty one. Already it showed signs of a poison. "First things first. Let's clean it out."

She poured water over it, cleaning it slowly and thoroughly. Green was impressed. Apparently, Wilson was too because he didn't fight her about fixing him. She tipped her head and locked gazes with Green. The blue in her eyes startled him each and every time he saw them. A bead of sweat trickled down her chest, disappearing between her breasts. His entire body tightened and the beast within wanted free. It cared little that they had an audience. All it wanted was to claim her. In truth, it was all the man in him wanted to do as well so it seemed right.

"Do you have iodine solution?"

Green was too busy fighting back his inner beast to answer her question. Jon bent down and searched the bag. He spent about a minute rifling through the bag's contents before snarling. "Shit, I packed this thing and forgot to put iodine in it. Sorry, Green, umm, Mel."

"That's fine. How about a lime? I've seen a good number of them around camp." Her soft voice worked wonders at chasing the beast within Green back enough to at least breathe normally. It did little for his erection, digging painfully into the zipper of his pants.

Putting his hand out, Eadan conjured a lime. "Here."

Wilson let out a nervous laugh. "That's a handy skill."

"Yeah, I'm a blast at parties," Eadan said with a wink. "If I knew where Jon left the iodine, I could probably call it forth, too."

Jon put his hand up. "I left it back in Virginia."

Eadan chuckled. "That's a wee bit far for me. Even I, Super-Eadan, can't do that."

Roi moved up next to them. "*Puleez*, tell me he'd didn't give himself superhero status."

Lukian appeared next to Roi. "We could get him a cape made. Some tights. The works. What do you think?"

Running a hand through his dark hair, Roi nodded. "Yeah, *blondie* would look good in tights. Super-Faerie. I'm afraid people might think he's a girl though."

Eadan did a rather fake yawn, patting his mouth as he went. "If only you could come up with some new potshots."

It was Wilson's turn to laugh. "Don't count on it, Eadan. The rat jokes never quit coming."

"Neither do I when I get started," Roi said, thrusting his hips, fucking nothing but air.

"I'm not supposed to bend over or anything, am I?" Eadan asked with a smirk on his face. Goading Roi seemed to be a favorite pastime of his. Roi seemed to enjoy it and in some warped way, it equaled bonding time for them so everyone let them go. "You've already confessed to thinking I'd look good in tights." Eadan winked.

"Are you coming onto to me or do you have something in your eye?" Roi folded his arms and clucked his tongue on his cheek. "You know, before I was married, I had a thing for blondes."

Eadan's face scrunched up. "Oh, you took it too far. I'm going to be sick now."

"Serves you right."

Eadan laughed. "I should take you up on the offer."

"Offer?" Roi snorted. "Please, you're so not my type."

Puckering his lips, Eadan made kissing noises and Wilson groaned. Melanie simply shook her head. "Boys, can we focus a moment here? I need a knife."

Jon handed her his knife. Melanie cut the lime in half and squeezed it over Wilson's open wound. Wilson jerked a bit and winced. It wasn't until Melanie grabbed the suture kit from the bag that Wilson finally commented. "Mels, I think the world of you, but I don't need stitches. I'll ... umm ... I'll heal this on my own."

She motioned towards the area surrounding Wilson's wound, paying extra attention to the darkened spots. "No you won't. See the way the skin is blackening around the edges?"

"Ye-ah?" Wilson asked, the tiniest hint of a squeak in his voice.

"Afraid your 'man-parts' are gonna fall off?" Roi clicked his fingers for added flare before cupping himself. "I'm secure and that's all that matters."

"Is he always this obnoxious?" Eadan asked.

Green stared at the man he hoped to one day have as a brother-in-law. "Unfortunately, yes."

Wilson growled as he stared at all of them. "Can we take a moment here and listen to what Mel has to say? I kind of like my 'man-parts' just where they are."

Melanie cast a pensive look at Wilson, making the were-rat's jaw drop. "Tell me nothing is gonna fall off, Mel."

Green tried to stifle his laugh and failed.

"I won't make any promises. If you're not a good little patient," she touched his knee, "things might just fall off. That or I'll rip them off."

Wilson gulped. So did Green. By the look of the men surrounding them cupping their groins, they all felt Wilson's pain.

Melanie giggled, sounding so much younger than she was, before taking a deep breath and composing herself. "They used a lead tipped-arrow, Wilson. When I shared my blood with you, it strengthened you when dealing with silver but weakened you to lead. While lead won't kill you, it will hurt like hell and your body will react this way. Now, let me stitch it up. We'll keep it clean and dry for a few days and you should be back to new." Sighing, her shoulders slumped. "Eadan and I can't heal lead wounds magikally very easily or we'd fix this for you that way. I'm sorry. Normally, at full strength, I could at least cut the healing time in half."

"Shh," Wilson whispered, reaching out and stroking her cheek. "Do what you have to. I trust you."

Green made a move to go at Wilson but found Jon and Roi pinning him in his place. He would have fought back but it was then he noticed Melanie begin stitching Wilson's wound closed. She was a pro and obviously knew what she was doing.

"Melanie, who taught you to do that?" Green asked.

She stiffened at the sound of his voice and that pained him greatly. "I spent my first three years of college double-majoring. I couldn't make up my mind between being a nurse practitioner or going more toward the science side of medicine. I opted for science but managed to come away with a number of useful skills."

"You told me you were studying fashion design," Eadan said, sounding shocked. It was hard for Green to hide his own surprise. He'd sensed Melanie was intelligent, never did he imagine how much.

"No," she let out a soft laugh, "I told you that when I graduate my degree will be in genetics and that I'm hoping to one day be a molecular geneticist. You were the one who thought I was joking and didn't believe me. I gave up and told you what you wanted to hear."

Jon let out a low whistle, leaning against a large tree trunk. His amber eyes lit with mischief. "She *is* tailor made for you, Green."

Melanie glanced back at Green. There was no mistaking the malice in her look. He'd hurt her and he knew it. "No. I'm not."

She went back to work, refusing to meet his gaze again. He couldn't let things continue the way they were going. He'd tried to give her space, time to calm down before he attempted to explain himself--or beg for her forgiveness. Whatever worked. Green bent down and touched her lower back. "I'm sorry."

"If you want me to kill him," Wilson glared at Green as he spoke to Melanie, "say the word."

Oh, he wants it to be that way, fine.

"I knocked you on your ass once over her, Wilson, don't think I won't do it again."

Roi let out a low whistle. "Stop bringing out the best in Green. I'm starting to think the guy's really a badass."

Melanie cupped Wilson's chin. The act was innocent yet it sent pangs of jealousy through Green. "I don't want Thad dead. I want him to be happy. He deserves as much."

"What about you, Mel?" Eadan asked, moving to his sister's side. He spun his hand in a circle and the air around him seemed to thicken. Melanie's hair lifted on the breeze Eadan magikally created and twisted into a loose bun. She didn't seem the least bit surprised, telling Green that regardless how much she and Eadan seemed to go at each other's throats, they loved one another and were close. "What about what you deserve?"

"The irony is that I got exactly what I deserve." She stood slowly.

Green reached for her but stopped just short of actually touching her. "No, you didn't deserve what I did, Melanie."

She stiffened, refusing to look in his direction and cutting him to the quick in the process. Melanie cleared her throat and nudged Wilson's good leg with her foot. "You need to avoid doing anything stupid that might tear it open for a couple of days. Can you handle that?"

Wilson slid his hand protectively over his groin and grinned. "If it'll keep anything from falling off, I'll do anything you tell me to."

"Men and their prized possessions," she mumbled as she took her brother's hand in hers.

Green didn't miss the gentle, reassuring squeeze she gave Eadan before looking around at everyone but him.

"I'm going to go wash my hands. I'm not like you guys. Blood does not excite me." Melanie laughed as she wandered down the path toward the river. All remaining eyes landed on Green.

He winced under the weight of their stare and put his hands up. "I know. I know. I was an asshole. I let the woman I love down and don't know how to fix it. There. I said it. I don't know how to fix this."

Lukian stepped forward. "Sometimes, the smartest men in the world have no common sense."

"Huh?"

"He's trying to tell you to pull your oversized intelligence out of your ass and do what your heart tells you to," Roi mused, picking up the bag. "Go find your future wife and don't leave her side until she knows how you feel about her. If that doesn't work, use that brain of yours to devise a way to hold her hostage until she--"

Lukian slapped Roi upside the back of his head and groaned.

Roi shrugged. "What?"

* * * *

Melanie rinsed her hands at the edge of the river and froze when she sensed someone watching her. As she turned and found a set of emerald eyes staring back at her, she did her best to hide her smile.

"You're happy to see me, I can sense it," Green said, his voice even.

She finished cleaning her hands and shook her head. "I'm not upset, if that's what you're asking. I'll be fine. Not that it matters."

"Not that it matters?" he echoed.

She gave him a pointed stare. "Our night together was fun. Nothing more. I think that with as sick as I've been and with all that's come to light recently, I was desperate to latch onto something--or in our case, someone. I realize what I was doing and am disgusted with my behavior."

"Melanie, don't sweep this under the rug because I hurt you." Green made a move to come to her but she backed away. "I have to admit that I was overwhelmed as well. That's no excuse for my behavior. I want to...."

Putting her hand up, she silenced him. "Really, Thad ... uh ... Green. It was what it was and it was fun. I'll give you one thing, you I-Op boys really can show a girl a good time." It was a low blow and she knew it. Watching Green stiffen and his jaw set should have made her feel vindicated. He'd hurt her more than she would ever admit by lying to her and she wanted him to understand how that felt. Throwing the fact that she'd fucked Lance too into the mix was the easiest way she could think to sweep his legs out from under him. It worked.

"Is that how you really feel?"

She snorted. "You tell me. I heard all about how you can sense truths."

Something she couldn't read moved over his face. He tipped his head. "I can't seem to read you the same way anymore, Melanie."

It was then that being out and about the majority of the day began to take its toll on her. Her hands cramped and her vision blurred slightly as pain tore through her. It felt as it someone had cracked her in the upper back with a sledgehammer. Melanie staggered and reached out to steady herself. The second her fingers skimmed over something warm she looked up to find Green standing there. He wrapped his large arms around her and held her close. She tried to push away from him but didn't have the strength.

"Shhh." He kissed the top of her head. "Let me love you, Melanie."

Let me love you?

Her chest tightened. "I want to go home, Green. I don't belong here."

"You belong with me." He caressed her back gently as he continued to hold her.

"No. I don't."

His lips brushed her neck and he purred every so slightly, sending need shooting throughout Melanie's body. She was tired and sore. No part of her should have craved sex yet she did. Not just sex but a primitive, hard fucking from Green to be exact. He swayed their bodies to a beat she didn't hear so much as she felt. The feel of his clothed erection pressing against her lower abdomen left Melanie panting and staring up into his emerald eyes.

"Don't," she whispered, unsure what exactly she wanted him to avoid doing.

His warm breath skated over her cheek, making her knees weak and her resolve crumble. Pushing on his chest, Melanie bit her lower lip. "Please, Thad, just go."

"I can't."

"Why?"

"Because I love you."

If shocking her to the point she was speechless was his goal, he'd succeeded nicely. Her brow knit as she tried and failed to soak in the magnitude of it all. The idea that a man as wonderful as Green could love her was too much for Melanie.

Push him away.
It can never work.
He'll break your heart.
Hurt you in ways you can't possibly imagine.
He can't love you for you, Melanie.

Her inner voice was relentless.

Green drew in a deep breath, seeming to savor her scent as he continued to rock their bodies. The moment he began to hum, Melanie melted in his arms. He chuckled as he kissed her cheek gently. "I want to touch you."

"You are touching me," she said, knowing full well what he meant.

He ran his hand down her arm, making her shiver with anticipation. The slow, sexy curve of Green's full lips left Melanie on the verge of moaning. "That I am."

She couldn't help but smile. "That you are."

"Forgive me." Green dipped her slightly and planted tiny kisses on her neck. "Please."

As much as she wanted to say no, that wasn't what came out. "I'll think about it."

"Green!"

The sound of Jon's voice snapped Melanie out of her sexual stupor. Green stood tall, taking Melanie with him and kept her close to him. Jon glanced at her and sighed. "I'm sorry. I didn't mean to interrupt but Captain needs both of you immediately."

"Jon?" Green kissed the top of her head. "What's wrong? Is it Wilson?"

"Negative. I don't know the details yet. All I know is that he wants you both, now. And I'm supposed to grab your medical supplies."

Green took her hand in his and she didn't protest. "Let's go."

Chapter Twelve

Green entered Melanie's hut, exhausted but needing to see her. They'd spent almost twenty-four hours treating native tribesmen suffering from symptoms of poisoning. In the end, it had been Melanie who suggested they dig deeper. When they did, everyone was shocked to find connections to Krauss' compound and the natives' sickness. They knew he was ruthless and would stop at nothing for the sake of science but attempting to wipe out a group of people for the simple fact that they were in the area was too much. Krauss' men had been so arrogant as to leave behind evidence in the form of containers of poisoning. Roi and Jon had found them near the natives food supply and had discovered it coated the majority of their cooking and drinking utensils.

The tribes' people were reluctant to allow them to treat them at first but Melanie and Eadan used their magik to calm them. They would live and that was all that mattered. Wilson had even managed to stop bitching about them being there long enough to find himself providing the entertainment for the children among them. Green still couldn't shake the visions of Wilson doing a sock puppet routine from his head. Thankfully, the children didn't speak English because Wilson wasn't exactly known for curbing his words. When Peren happened upon him having one puppet "kick the living shit" out of the other, she slapped him in the back of the head and the children roared with laughter.

The entire group of I-Ops and their mates found themselves the guests of honor at a celebration. The natives went out of their way to thank them for all they'd done. It wasn't necessary. Standing idly by and letting Krauss get away with murder wasn't an option. Green shuddered to think of Krauss' motives for getting rid of the tribes. It wasn't as if they understood genetics or how to be international evil geniuses. They were simple in a way that left them appreciating life, their loved ones and each day they were given. Krauss' ability to put his thumb to the artery of the innocent, sickened Green.

Innocent.

Green stared down at Melanie as she slept in the bed. Mosquito netting covered her nearly nude frame. Long strands of white-blonde hair fanned out around her in a halo-like effect. She'd left Green no choice but to yell at her to go and rest. Her dedication to helping the tribe was unrivaled. It was then he realized she was more than capable of loving and caring, she just didn't know it. She'd worked next to him the entire day, seeming to read his every thought--so attuned to him that for a moment, it was hard to imagine his life before she was in it.

Green's shoulders had begun to ache mid-way through the day and Melanie slid around him, rubbing the kinks away without him ever mentioning they hurt. She also stopped him throughout the day, insisting he replenish his fluids by drinking lots of water. The concern in her voice had been genuine and the love in her eyes unmistakable.

Pulling his sweat-soaked shirt off, Green debated on going to the river to freshen up before crawling into bed with Melanie. His body ached to be near hers and he needed to sleep. She deserved better than to have a stinky man trying to cuddle close to her. He laid his shirt over the back of a chair, near a rather flimsy desk and stared back at Melanie. He turned to head out and stopped when she whimpered.

"No, Elizabeth, I won't leave him," she whispered, still asleep.

Green's chest tightened.

"I know he's hurt me but I can't go. Don't you understand that I can't walk away from him? He doesn't think I know he spends his nights with me. I do. I wake feeling his arms around me and know I'm safe with him--that I can rest knowing Thad will be there until morning."

She knows?

Green edged closer to her, afraid to try to wake her for fear of what it might to do her. He'd bore witness to one of her moving from plane to plane and saw what it took out of her. If there was even a remote chance that Melanie wasn't dreaming, but was on the other plane, truly speaking to the portion of herself that was Elizabeth, Green didn't want to chance ripping her from it.

"Elizabeth, I've never wanted a man to stay with me, to never let me go. I want that with Thad. I want him to look at me the way Lukian looks at Peren. The way Roi watches Missy. I can't explain it. I just know I do." Melanie shook her head slightly, still asleep. A smile spread over her face. "He told me he loves me today."

"And I do," Green whispered, pushing the netting back and sliding into bed with her. He kissed her temple and moved her hair to avoid laying on it. Her smell was intoxicating and the urge to taste her great. "I love you so much, honey. I'm sorry I didn't tell you the truth. I was shocked you were happy with the idea of being my wife."

Melanie snuggled against him but didn't wake. She skimmed her soft hand down his stomach and dipped her fingers down the front of his pants. Green's cock responded by going painfully erect. He hissed as she wrapped her long fingers around his shaft.

"Melanie, honey, wake up."

She didn't. Instead, Melanie caressed him, stroking his cock as she pressed her body to his. His body was as starved for her as he was but the idea of making love to her when she wasn't awake didn't sit well with him. He nudged her slightly and kissed her neck. "Wake up, baby."

Melanie went rigid and for a moment Green thought she'd kick him out of her room. When she continued to stroke his cock, he relaxed and kissed her temple once more. "Hey, honey, I didn't mean to wake you but...."

"It's fine," she said, her voice sounding oddly like Elizabeth's.

A chill ran over Green and he pulled Melanie closer to him. "Mel?"

"I want you in me." She tugged on his shaft, her grip bordered on painful.

"Melanie? Honey?"

"Don't you want me? I used to be good enough, Thaddy," she said, this time leaving no doubt in his mind that she sounded identical to Elizabeth.

Green touched her shoulder gently and found it hard to breathe as the reality of it all began to sink in. Had the merger taken place? If so, did Elizabeth now control the woman he loved.

You love Elizabeth, too.

He nodded as his inner thoughts filled his head. It was true. He did love Elizabeth and according to her own words, she and Melanie were one in the same but Green knew better. Melanie felt different to him. She was her own identity, separate from Elizabeth's or at least she had been.

"Come on, Thaddy, don't you want to fuck me anymore?"

His blood ran cold. Something was wrong. Not only did Melanie's voice sound like Elizabeth's but she was saying things his Elizabeth would never have dreamt to utter. As gray eyes stared out at him in place of Melanie's blue ones, Green gasped and grabbed her shoulders. "What the hell is going on?"

She licked her lower lip and smiled wickedly. "I've come back, Thaddy. I'm home. Now, fuck me."

He scrambled out of the bed, getting temporarily caught up in the netting as he did. "Where's Melanie?"

"Only one could keep the body, Thaddy. Only one." She held a finger up for emphasis. "Why don't you look happier to have me back? Is it because you loved her more? You wanted to bite her, claim her as your life mate. You never had the urge to do that to me."

"Elizabeth, please. I need to know Melanie's okay. You're not acting like yourself. Please." He put his hands up and tipped his head. "I just need to know that...."

She stood quickly and eyed him like a snake about to strike. "You just have to know if your precious bitch is nearby. If she can hear what's going on." A sly smile crept over her face. "She is and she can but I won't let her up. Not just yet. I'm holding her place until...."

"I arrive," a deep voice said from the other side of the room.

Green turned to find Ferdian there, leaning against the wall leisurely. He didn't waste time talking. No. Green charged him, the need to tear his head off was too great to resist. He swept out, letting his hands shift, claws lengthen and the beast partially up. It felt like a truck hitting him, lifted him off the ground and slammed him back down onto it.

Ferdian laughed. "You are no match for me, Thaddy." He put his hand out. "Come, Elizabeth. Bring me her body so that he may die knowing I took pleasure in both the women he loved."

"Don't you fucking touch her!" Green watched in horror as Ferdian drew Melanie into his arms and ran his fingers down her neck. "Melanie, no!"

She jerked slightly and for a moment, he hoped to have gotten through to her on some level.

Levels. Planes. That's it.

Closing his eyes, Green concentrated on Melanie. The thought of her blue eyes. Her smile. The way she cared for the tribes' people. The way she made his chest tight by simply being near him.

Melanie, I need you. I need to know you're okay.

Something tugged at his consciousness and he blinked to find himself standing in the meadow he'd first seen Melanie and Elizabeth together in. It was dark and thunder boomed all around him. Wind whipped past and he caught the slightest flicker of blonde in the distance. He ran full force towards it, coming to a grinding halt as he found himself face to face with Elizabeth.

"Where is she?" he bit out, fury consuming him.

Elizabeth shook her head as tears filled her eyes. "I'm so sorry, Thad. I am. Jealousy consumed me and I did it." She averted her gaze. "I weakened her to the point Ferdian's magik could affect her."

Confused, Green shook his head. "Why are you letting him touch her--you?"

"When I submitted to Ferdian, magikally, and let him begin to weaken Melanie from a distance. I also gave up my ability to resist his evil."

"Are you here now to try to stop me from finding her?" He wasn't sure what to say about Elizabeth giving into Ferdian.

"No. I'm here to help you find her. This is the little bit of my essence that Ferdian hasn't soiled. Once he has managed to change me completely, I won't be able to stop myself from attacking Melanie's essence, Thad."

He drew in a sharp breath. "You'll kill her ... You'll kill yourself?"

"Thad, I died long ago. The wall erected to separate our essences allowed Melanie to grow into her own person. I have been here to guide her when I can but for the most part, I remained hidden. It wasn't until you came into her life that I dared to interact with her emotions." She looked away, shame covering her face. "I was jealous of how quickly you took to her. How intense your feelings for her are. And the minute I sensed you fighting the urge to claim her, I forced Melanie to push power out and over you to prevent it."

"Elizabeth," he whispered, disappointed in her. "You were the only woman in my life until she entered it and in the end she was you. At least a part of her was. How could you be...."

"Jealous that it would never be me having eternity with you? That it wouldn't be me giving birth to your children, loving you forever?"

Moved by the truth in her words and the emotion on her face, Green went to embrace her. She shook her head and put her hand up. "No, Thad. Your heart is big but I know the truth in it. You love Melanie like you have never loved another. The truth of the matter is, it was always her who was intended to be with you. I think I somehow knew that and that's why I magikally pushed Tatiana from the ether to try for another child after Eadan. It's why I forced myself to be part of Melanie. I knew she was destined to be yours and part of me hoped I would be allowed to live her life-- truly be yours."

"I'm sorry," he whispered.

She cleared her throat and wiped tears from her cheeks. "You loved me as much as you could considering you were my true mate but I wasn't yours, Thad. It's rare but it's been known to happen. Still, you mourned me for fifty years. I gave up my immortality and thus, my ability to carry your children to term. Yet, you blame yourself. Don't apologize for that. What I do need is for you to fight for her. To refuse to give up on her." She took a deep breath. "Claim her as soon as you can. It will give you more power to fight Ferdian. It will take many of you to bring him down but it can be done."

Green rubbed his face and sighed. "I'm going to lose her. I can feel it."

"Dammit, Thad," Elizabeth said sharply. "Pull yourself together and go to her. She's terrified right now and doesn't trust me to let me close to her. I can't blame her. What you see before you is all that is pure, untainted by Ferdian and it's fading fast."

"If we defeat Ferdian, will you still kill her?"

She gulped. "What is consuming my essence is pure evil. It will not rest until it's vanquished from her, Thad. You have to hurry. Melanie's weakened right now and the baby is too new to survive her current state."

"Baby?" Green's brow furrowed. "Lance didn't get her pregnant. She can't conceive with anyone but me."

Elizabeth arched a brow and then smiled wide. "For a smart man, you seem incapable of thinking clearly when it comes to her." She pointed at him. "You're the baby's father, Green. It's nearing a week old within her."

His heart hammered within his chest. "That's why I'm having trouble reading her. Why I ... oh gods ... she's pregnant with my child." He drew in a sharp breath and backed away. "No! I won't lose her, too. I won't watch her die trying to give birth to my child."

Elizabeth pointed to the east. "Thad, she was destined to be your mate, the mother of your children and the woman you love for eternity. She's immortal. She's powerful enough to carry your children to term and be with you forever. Find her. Claim her as you know you want to and protect her from Ferdian and from me. Go!"

He took no time in rushing off in the direction Elizabeth pointed. Within seconds, he found Melanie lying in a fetal position as wind whipped around her, tugging at her long blonde hair. "Melanie!"

She lifted her head slightly and looked at him. "Go away! You're not Green. I won't believe your lies."

"Melanie, look at me. Really look at me."

She did and her eyes widened. "Green?"

In an instant he had her swept up into his arms and cradled close to his chest. "Gods, honey, I'm so sorry. I love you. I do. With all my heart."

She leaned her cheek against his chest. "No. Your heart belongs to Elizabeth and I'm not her. I never will be."

"I know that you're not her and you're wrong." He held her close and began to run with her, unsure where exactly he was going. "I do love you. You're my true mate. Not Elizabeth. You." His gaze slid down to her midriff. "We're going to be a family, Melanie."

She clung to him and began to cry. "I can feel him, Green. He's about to," she sobbed, "have sex with me ... with my body. I can't control it. I can't stop him."

Anger tore through him. He growled and lost control of himself. The next thing he knew, he had set Melanie down and shifted into full panther form. In an instant he was back in the room in South America, on the floor, this time in shifted form. He looked over to see Ferdian shoving Melanie against the wall, lifting her flimsy nightgown over her hips and reaching for his own pants. He roared in cat form and pounced, catching Ferdian off guard and sinking his teeth deep into the man's arm.

Green clawed out, ripping Ferdian's upper chest open and knocking him away from Melanie. He went to strike again, this time to tear open Ferdian's throat but the man vanished into thin air. The smell of his blood lingered as the taste of it filled Green's mouth.

* * * *

Melanie's head spun and she fought to stay upright as she suddenly found herself pressed against the wall of her room. She looked down to find a black panther in the center of her room. Its mouth was covered in blood and it looked crazed. The sound of someone screaming caught her attention. It took her a minute to realize she was the one doing screaming.

The door to her room burst open. Eadan appeared, looking ready to kill someone or something. His gaze went to the black panther. "You hurt her?" He raised his hands as the panther suddenly begin to shift forms, morphing into a man. Not just any man--Green.

A second before Eadan would have released his power, Melanie shot forward, putting her body in front of Green's. "No! He saved me!"

Eadan put his hands down. "Saved you?"

"Ferdian was here. He tried to--" She glanced at Green, searching for the right words.

Green, seemingly unaffected by the fact he was naked, locked gazes with Eadan. "He tried to rape her."

"He did what?" Eadan's power buzzed around the room, no doubt searching for something or someone to destroy.

She ran to Green and he pulled her into his arms protectively. Shaking her head she clung to him. "I couldn't stop her. I couldn't stop Elizabeth."

"Shh," he stroked her hair, "I know, honey. I know."

"What happened with Elizabeth?" Eadan asked, sounding lost.

Anger surged through Green and something deep within him began to build. Pushing it down, he focused on holding Melanie in his arms. His gaze slid to Eadan's. "Unless you want to stay and watch me claim your sister as my wife, I strongly suggest…."

Eadan looked as if he was going to be sick. "I'm going! I'm not going far so try to be quiet. I really *do not* want to hear anything!" He shut the door and Green twisted Melanie to face him.

Her blue eyes were filled with unshed tears. "I'm going to claim you."

"You don't want me, Green. It's okay. I understand. I…."

Running his hand up her back and into her hair, he tugged gently, forcing her gaze to stay locked on him. He growled. "I didn't ask, Melanie. I'm telling you. I'm going to claim you. I'm going to sink my cock and teeth into you until there is no question in your mind that you, and only you, belong to me."

He lifted her off her feet and carried her to the bed. He set her down, facing away from him and kissed her bare shoulder. "Get on your hand and knees."

She glanced over her shoulder and gave him a questioning look. The last thing he wanted to do was claim her after what Ferdian had just attempted but he needed to protect her and claiming her would help. In truth, he wanted her as his mate and the beast within could wait no longer.

He moved up behind her, his cock hardening at the sight of her lush ass bent up for the offering. The tiny silk nightgown she wore, without panties, slid higher, exposing the globes of her ass. He fought the urge to growl.

"Don't be scared, Melanie. I love you and I know how scared of me you were when you saw me in shifted form." He motioned for her to look ahead. "I'll enter you and I'll bite your shoulder. The combination of me taking your blood in the heat of passion and coming in you marks you as mine--as my mate, as my wife."

Her eyes widened. "You're going to shift into a panther and fuck me?"

A manly chuckle escaped him. "No, honey. My teeth will shift and possibly," his gaze slid lower, over his cock, "another area may increase but that's all. Not full cat. I promise."

She didn't look comforted by his attempts at reassurance. "Thad, your cock is already so big I can barely take it all. I can't fit any more in me. I can't...."

Manly pride swelled in him as he wagged his brows. Licking his fingers, he let saliva build on them before coating his dick with it. He stood, butted against the side of the bed and aligned perfectly with Melanie. He nudged the entrance of her wet pussy with the head of his cock. "I'll do my best to maintain control, honey. I promise. But you have to promise *not* to use your magik to control my beast. We have to let nature take its course, honey."

"I ... I promise."

He slapped her ass cheek playfully and then rubbed the area. "You're mine, Melanie. Mine and mine alone. Understand?"

The grin that spread over her sexy face told him she not only understood but enjoyed what he was doing. He gave her other cheek a tiny slap. His cock grew painfully erect and he gave into the urge to be in her. He thrust to the hilt and she cried out. Lacing his fingers into the back of her hair, Green held tight as he began pumping in and out of her. Her pussy clenched around him, doing its best to keep him locked within her silken depths. Green didn't fight nature. He let his mouth shift, his teeth lengthen and could do little to stop the fact that his cock swelled as well.

Melanie gasped and moaned, clutching the bed as Green continued to pummel her body, taking them both close to culmination. "Mine," he ground out between his shifted teeth as he leaned over her, rooting his cock in her. He bit down on her shoulder, savoring the coppery sweet taste of her blood. It washed away the taste of Ferdian's blood.

"Yes, Green! Yes!" Melanie arched her back. "I'm coming. Come with me!"

He didn't need to be told twice. His balls drew up and seed jetted from his body into hers as he continued to drink from her. When he lifted his mouth from her shoulder, he licked the wound and it healed over instantly. Lifting his wrist to his mouth, he stayed rooted deep in her womb as he bit through his own flesh. Blood welled and he reached around, putting his wrist before Melanie. Since she wasn't a shifter, he wasn't sure if she would have the same desire to exchange blood during the mating process.

Her tongue darted out and over his bleeding wrist. She licked it and moaned. "Mine, Green. You belong to me and me alone. No other."

His wrist healed over instantly. Allowing his mouth to shift back to normal, he planted tiny kisses on her shoulders. "That's right, honey. I'm yours and you're mine--forever."

"Mmm, now do me a favor and lessen that cock a bit. I think I'm going to rip in two." She squirmed a bit.

Laughing, Green did as his wife instructed, focusing on returning his cock to its normal size.

My wife.

The thought warmed him as withdrew from her and went to turn her. Melanie shook her head and let out a sultry laugh. "Oh, no way are you stopping. You're back there and have got me so horny I can barely stand it." She wiggled her ass, causing his still erect cock to slip along the cleft and nearly enter her anus. "Mmm, yes."

"Yes?" he asked, slightly confused.

Melanie reached back, took hold of his cock, rubbed it in their combined juices and aligned it with her ass. "Take all of me, Green. I have a feeling the beast within you would enjoy it greatly. And I'm positive I would too."

His heart thumped madly as the carnal need to lay claim to the tiny rosette before him besieged him. He'd never taken a woman that way. Unable to stop himself, Green eased into her anus slightly. It was tight, so tight he almost came with nothing more than the tip of his dick in her. Grinding his teeth, he pushed in more, scared of hurting her.

Melanie thrust back against him, taking his cock deep. She cried out and for a second he thought he hurt her. When she began rocking back, fucking him with her ass, he knew better. She liked it and wanted more.

Reaching around, he slid his finger over her clit and rubbed it, taking her to new heights as he continued the sweet assault of her ass. "Ah, yes, Melanie. Yes."

"Fuck me harder. Harder."

He did. He lost control, coming in waves into her, filling her completely. Melanie shuddered beneath him as an orgasm ripped through her. She flung her head back and locked gazes with him. "Bite me again. I liked it."

Chuckling, Green wagged his brows and obeyed. "Yes, wife," he said, letting his mouth shift slightly before sinking his teeth into her shoulder once again.

Melanie cried out, coming so hard that her ass gripped his shaft, refusing to allow him to move. Giving in, Green stayed in her warmth, savoring the feel of her body and the taste of her blood.

I love you.

"Mmm," Melanie murmured. "I want to get cleaned up and then...."

He licked the bite mark, healing it over almost instantly. "And then what?"

Her seductive gaze told him all. "I want to play more with you, Thad."

He withdrew from her slowly and grinned like a kid in a candy store. "Mmm, play with me? Hmm, I think I could set time aside for you."

Her jaw dropped. "Some time?"

"Mmmhmm," he whispered in a teasing manner. "And if you promise to recite the periodical chart, I might even...."

Her power wrapped around him quickly, lifting him off the bed. Green laughed as Melanie wagged her little finger. "Oh, you want to play like that, huh?"

He winked and Melanie's cheeks flushed. It was adorable. As was she. "I love you."

She pointed down and her power cradled around him, lowering him to the floor gently. "Race you to the river."

"What about your brother?" Green asked, remembering Eadan's warning of staying in the area.

Melanie's blue gaze went to his cock. "I think he got an eyeful when he walked in."

"Yes, but he didn't see you naked."

She snorted. "Very true. He'd have poked his eyes out if he had."

With a wave of her hand, Melanie had towels wrapped around them, covering any parts the public shouldn't be exposed to.

Chapter Thirteen

Melanie giggled as Green pressed his body against hers. He had pants and boots on but hadn't bothered with a shirt, allowing his muscular upper body to show. "Stop that."

"No."

She continued towel drying her hair and laughing as he rubbed his body against hers. "I can't get enough of you."

Wiggling slightly, she grinned. "I know. You're worse than me. I'm actually sore. Can you believe that? I'm too sore to have sex with you."

Green pressed his forefinger to her lips. "No. Make love, Melanie. That's what we do. No matter how heated, how carnal it is, we make love."

She smiled, liking the sound of that. "Yes. We make love." Staring back into his emerald eyes, Melanie reached over her shoulder and cupped his cheek. "I think I'm in love with you."

His lips quivered as he if were trying not to laugh. "You think, huh? Hmm, what can I do to persuade you? I could spend the next two days licking every sore spot on your body and I do mean *every* spot."

"I would marry a man who is insatiable." She kissed his jaw and leaned into his embrace. "What are we going to do about Ferdian and Elizabeth?"

"*You* aren't going to a thing. You're going to get plenty of rest and take care of yourself."

"Thad, you can't go up against...."

He stiffened and the buzz of energy surrounded her. It was Ferdian's but it wasn't. Power lashed out and whirled around her before striking a tree, and snapping branches from it. She yelped.

Green loosened his hold on her. "Shit."

That doesn't sound good.

"Thad?" She turned and faced him. Her skin was still damp from bathing with Green in the river so her fitted t-shirt stuck to her.

"Get Eadan! Now!"

"Thad?" She shook her head. "It wasn't Ferdian. It felt like his power but it wasn't him."

"I know," he whispered. "It was me, Melanie. I don't understand how or why but it was--" He stopped and his eyes widened. "I bit him. His blood. Your blood." In an instant, he whirled around and rushed down the trail back to camp.

Melanie ran behind him, unsure what was going on. As they broke through the line of trees, Green rushed at Wilson who was lounging in a hammock, with his injured leg raised.

"Green, no! You'll rip his stitches!" Melanie shouted, trying to grab hold of him but missing.

Wilson jerked awake and put his hands up as if to say I'm innocent. "I didn't touch her, Green. I swear. I thought about it." He shrugged as a lazy sly grin spread over his face. "What guy wouldn't?"

Green shook his head. "What the hell are you talking about?"

Wilson glanced back at Melanie and sighed. "Good. Please tell him I never touched you. He looks like he wants to rip my head off."

Melanie laughed. "My husband's lost his mind, Wilson."

"Husband?" His eyes widened. "Oh, shit, he did it! He finally claimed you!"

She nodded and Wilson tried to come to her quickly, hissing as pain went through his leg. Green grabbed hold of Wilson's Hawaiian shirt. "You mentioned that other things, weird things you didn't want to talk about were going on with you. What are they?"

Wilson suddenly looked shifty eyed, seeming to go out of his way to avoid looking in Melanie's direction. "Nothing."

Green growled. "Lie to anyone else, rat. It won't fly with me. What the hell changed?"

Wilson bit his lower lip. "After, *your* wife," he glanced at Melanie, "kissed me. I didn't kiss her, remember that. After she kissed me and pushed her blood into my mouth, strange shit started happening."

"Like?" Green pressed on.

Wilson groaned. "Like I woke up levitating off my bed while stuff in my room moved around like something out of *Fantasia*. Minus the music and cute mouse." He blinked innocently. "I like to think of myself as a sexy rat, rather than an adorable mouse."

Releasing Wilson, Green began mumbling to himself as he paced in a circle. He stopped and grinned from ear to ear. A look she wasn't used to seeing on him. It seemed almost childish. "Do you realize what's happened?"

Melanie shook her head.

"Somehow, by ingesting your blood and Ferdian's, the two of you transferred Fae magik to me." He pointed at Wilson. "You did the same to him." He growled. "You won't be kissing him again though. Understand?"

She bit her inner cheek in an attempt to not laugh. "Understood."

"What's going on?" Roi asked, rounding the corner and coming to a halt. "You going to kill Wilson and not let the rest of us watch?"

Green seemed to think about it for a moment.

Melanie rushed forward, putting her body in front of Wilson's. "No! He's not going to kill Wilson."

Wilson put his hands on her hips and his forehead on her side, still lying in the hammock. He sighed. "Thanks, Mels."

Green cocked his head to the side, looking deadly. "Get your hands off my wife."

"Your wife?" Roi asked. "You did it? You claimed her?"

"Yes," Green said, his gaze piercing Melanie's soul. "I love her more than I've ever loved anything in my life and I refuse to let her slip through my grasp."

Melanie blushed.

Roi tipped his head back and cupped his hands around his mouth. "Green did it! The Genius finally fucking claimed Melanie!"

Within seconds, the rest of the I-Ops along with Peren and Missy appeared. The men took turns punching Green's upper arm and congratulating him on finally "getting off his ass." Peren and Missy embraced Melanie, holding her tight.

Eadan came at her fast and the girls moved aside. He lifted her in the air and bounced her around. "Never, ever did I think my little sister would settle down. Not only did you, but you did it with a man I trust fully."

"Don't rough house with her, Eadan. She's weak and the baby's already hanging on by...."

Everyone, including Melanie, fell silent. It was Peren who spoke first. "Baby? I thought Eadan said Melanie wasn't pregnant with Lance's child."

Green's gaze remained on Melanie as he answered, "She's not expecting Lance's child. She's carrying my child--our child."

Shocked to the core, Melanie pushed on her brother's shoulders until he set her back onto her feet. She shook her head, unable to believe what Green had just said. She blinked and then pointed at him, anger taking hold of her. "I told you that if you sneezed by me I'd end up pregnant! I warned you that I'm not cut out to be a mother. I'm so far from…."

Green smiled and she wanted to throw something at him. "Honey, you are the most caring woman I know. I love you and…."

She took a step back. "No! No talk of love when I want to throw something heavy at your head."

Roi chuckled. "Use Wilson. Toss that Fae power around him and catapult his ass at Green. Let me make popcorn first though."

Jon laughed, something she didn't hear him do too often. "Put extra butter on it and grab napkins. I want to watch too."

Lukian lowered his head and shook slightly, no doubt laughing as well.

Melanie put her hands on her hips and gave them all a hard look. "This is not funny!"

Pushing past the others, Green smiled slyly before putting his arms out to her. "It's hilarious, honey. Now, come here. I want to hold you."

She wanted to be mad at him but it was impossible. His emerald eyes flickered and she found herself going into his arms and hugging him. "I'm still mad at you."

"I can live with that," he whispered. "So long as you still love me."

"I do."

Wilson made a gagging noise. "Do we have to listen to this? Really, everyone and their brother are shackling themselves to women lately. Is it something in the air? Should Eadan, Jon and I put on respirators to avoid catching it?"

Melanie knew Wilson was attempting to lighten the mood but still, the fear of motherhood, of Ferdian and Elizabeth consumed her. She clung to Green. When his powerful arms wrapped around her, she felt safe, loved and protected.

Chapter Fourteen

Wilson sat on a stool at the end of the kitchen of the compound and watched the women as they each chopped something or other. They were currently gossiping about babies, who out of the people they knew was a mother already. The topic of conversation held no interest to him so he sat there, sharpening his knife. Part of him was nervous that if he actually paid attention, he'd somehow catch "it"--as impossible as it sounded.

"Wilson?" Melanie asked, jarring Wilson from his thoughts. "Did you hear me?"

"Huh?" he asked, fisting his knife.

She smiled and held a plate out to him. "I asked if you were hungry."

He glanced down at the food as his stomach growled. Fresh fruit, cooked fish, some sort of green stuff--it looked delicious, even if he wasn't entirely sure what it all was. "I am. Thanks."

"No problem. Oh, Peren, can you and Missy go check on the two tribesmen who are left in the infirmary? I'm not sure when Green and the others will be back from whatever the hell is they've decided to do now."

Peren laughed. "You get used to it, Melanie."

"Sure, we'll check on them," Missy said, laughing as she led Peren out.

The minute they left the room, Melanie took the plate from his hand and began to move her hips seductively. Wilson reached for his plate. "Mels, what are you doing? I'm hungry and a little shocked you can cook."

She began to unbutton the tiny pair of tan shorts she wore and his mouth went dry. "I'm giving you what you're really hungry for, Wilson."

Her voice sounded different. Very different. Not only that, but her scent had changed.

"Mels?" He shifted uncomfortably on the chair and let out a nervous laugh. "Ha, ha, fun is over. My luck, Green will walk in while you're trying to be amusing. Trust me when I say, his sense of humor doesn't extend to this. I already pushed his limits at the restaurant, when I said all of that crap about you to get him riled up. The guy can throw a punch. I don't want to know what it feels like to have him really gunning for me."

"Oh," she took hold of his hand and shoved it under her t-shirt, "I'm not being funny, Wilson. I want you in me. Green will never find out."

Shocked, Wilson stared up at her. It was then he noticed her normally blue eyes were gray. "Melanie?"

She ground her body against him, squeezing his hand which in turn left him kneading her breast. The next thing he knew, she had her lips pressed to his and her tongue thrust into his mouth. She yanked hard on him, causing him to flip off the stool and tumble onto her. They hit the floor with a thud. The knife he'd been sharpening stuck into the floor, narrowly missing Melanie's head. Wilson gasped and tried to get off her. An unseen force held him there, pressing him to her. It took hold of his hips, grinding them against her lean body. As confused as he was, he was still a man, a man currently lying on top of a gorgeous woman. His cock hardened and the unseen force continued to press him against Melanie's body.

Melanie pushed on his chest. "No, Wilson. Stop, Green's my mate, not you," she said, her voice still sounding nothing like her own. The pressure in the air surrounding him reached new heights, drawing his mind back to the fact something very wrong was going on.

"Huh? What? Mels? I didn't...."

Pain seared through his body as something ripped him up and off Melanie. The deep growl near his ear alerted him to who was there--Green. "I didn't...."

Green threw him against the wall. Wilson hit it hard, pain radiating through his head. "I asked you to watch over her. Not to force yourself on my wife!"

Wilson put his hands up, doing his best to explain what was happening. Green focused on him, his back to Melanie. The moment that Wilson spotted his long-time friend's eyes beginning to swirl, he knew he was in deep shit.

A flash of silver appeared behind Green's back. When Green's eyes widened, Wilson knew what he saw was not imaginary. Melanie had stabbed Green in the back.

Green fell to his knees next to Wilson, looking as confused as Wilson felt.

"Melanie stabbed you," Wilson said, pushing to his feet, ignoring the pain in his leg. "Her smell is different. Her eyes aren't blue anymore, they're gray and she's nuts."

Green grabbed his good leg and Wilson thought for sure he'd rip it off. "Melanie's not in control of herself. Don't hurt her. It's Elizabeth. Not her."

Wilson glanced at Melanie and found her licking the bloody knife. A smile came over her. "He really is a genius, isn't he?"

"Leave her alone, Elizabeth," Green said, sounding winded.

"Green, you okay?" Wilson asked.

Melanie laughed. "I imagine he's in some pain. I did just pierce his lung. That has to hurt." She lifted the knife. "Wait and see what happens when I pierce his heart."

Melanie's eyes flickered to blue and she screamed, throwing the knife far in the other direction. "No! I won't let you hurt them!"

Now that sounded like Melanie's voice.

She screamed once more and went to her knees. Her body contorted and the next thing Wilson knew, a blonde woman seemed to roll right out of Melanie's body. This one looked as if she could be Mel's sister. Her eyes were gray though and she was shorter than Mel. His eyes widened. "Elizabeth?"

The woman next to Melanie pushed to her feet. "Wilson, so nice to finally meet you face to face, without this bitch interfering." She kicked Melanie in the chest.

Wilson went to charge her and she threw power at him, sending him hurdling into the air. Green seized hold of him a second before he would have struck the wall again. The second Green let go of Wilson he charged Elizabeth. He tackled her, taking her over the top of the table and crashing onto the floor with her.

Rushing to Melanie's side, Wilson smoothed her hair from her face. "Mels? Mels, can you hear me?"

She didn't budge. Deciding it was best to get her to the others to watch over while he grabbed Eadan to help fight another Fae, Wilson lifted her into his arms and ran as quickly as he could.

He made it about three steps out of the kitchen building when he found himself surrounded by a circle of men carrying automatic weapons. Each one was trained on him. A tall man with long black hair stepped forward. Wilson didn't need to be told who the guy was. Eadan had done a great job jarring Wilson's memory. The man was Ferdian.

"Give her to me and only you die. Continue to hold her and you sentence her to death as well."

Melanie was his friend, the only friend he'd had outside of the I-Ops and he couldn't allow harm to come to her. His options were limited. One thing was for sure, he had no doubt Ferdian would kill her if he kept hold of her. Reluctantly, Wilson handed Melanie over to Ferdian carefully.

The second he backed away, shots rang out. It felt as if his body was on fire as he crumbled to the ground. Darkness swept in around him as he felt people lifting him into the air.

* * * *

Melanie woke slowly, her head aching and her chest feeling as if she'd been struck with a bat. She moaned as she opened her eyes and sunlight hit them.

"Ah, there you are. I was wondering when you'd awaken."

She froze. "Ferdian?"

Turning, she realized she was in a bed, near a window and that Ferdian was lying next to her. She went rigid and he laughed, running his hand over her bare back. For a moment, Melanie thought she was naked. It wasn't until his hand skimmed over her ass that she realized she was in some sort of long skirt. She glanced down and exhaled as she found her breasts contained in a bra-like white top.

Ferdian chuckled and pressed his mouth to her ear. "Oh, fear not, Melanie. I want you awake when I enter you. I'm guessing sex with you will be divine."

She drew in a sharp breath.

"I can sense your fear. I'll be gentle." He laughed. "At first."

"I won't let you touch me," she said, unsure what exactly she could do to stop him but knowing she'd never willingly submit to him.

"Oh, I think you will." He nudged her and pointed toward the end of the bed. In the back corner there was a slumped figure. A figure she knew well--Green. Elizabeth was next to him, jerking his head up and slapping his bloody face.

"Wake! Watch your mate give herself to another, Thaddy. See what a whore she truly is. See what you forsake me for."

Green blinked and then opened his swollen eyes. His emerald eyes locked on Melanie and she tried to run to him. Ferdian snaked his arm around her waist and yanked her back to him.

"Shame, shame. Trying to run out on your commitment, Melanie." He pinched her breast and pain went through it. "For that, you will be punished."

"No," Green said, his voice barely above a whisper.

Ferdian laughed. "Please, you cannot stand up to me. Hell, you cannot even stand on your own two feet at the moment. You got lucky the last time. It won't happen again." He flicked his wrist. "Elizabeth, you may play with him. I fully intend to enjoy her, so you may as well enjoy one last time with the bastard before I kill him."

The idea of Elizabeth touching Green intimately enraged Melanie. Her power began to build.

Ferdian ran his hand over her lower abdomen. "Please know, Dr. Thaddeus Green, that I will be keeping her as my wife and that your child will be raised as my own, never having any knowledge of you."

Elizabeth's gaze shot to him and Melanie could see the jealousy in her eyes. Deciding now was as good as time as any, Melanie fought back. Her first weapon of choice, words and sexual prowess. She smiled. "What's wrong, *Aunt* Elizabeth? Upset you're being replaced by a younger model?"

Laughing, Ferdian pulled her against him, rubbing the length of his body against hers. "Mmm, I knew it wasn't all an act. I can smell the sex nymph in you, Melanie. It desires a Fae lover, as do I."

"You already have a Fae lover, Ferdian," Elizabeth said, her voice harsh. Jealousy gleamed in her eyes. "You said you wanted to make Green think you were going to fuck his precious wife before you slit her throat in front of his eyes. You told me you'd kill him too and that we'd…."

"That we would what, Elizabeth?" Ferdian laughed. "Ride off into the sunset? You are alive because my power wills it. You're not truly back. Not unless you take Melanie's body as your own but you weren't strong enough to do that, were you? She pushed you out. As much as I enjoyed having you around all those years ago, I got my revenge on you for leaving me. In fact, I will continue getting it every time I sink my dick into Melanie and make her scream my name as she comes. You got your wish, Elizabeth, you are rid of me. I have found a replacement for you." He put his hand on Melanie's chin and she bent her head to suck on his finger.

It sickened her but it was necessary for him to believe she would have him. "Mmm."

"No!" Elizabeth shrieked. "You lie! You swore!"

"Oh, come off it, Elizabeth. Green replaced you with Melanie as will I. Face it, you just don't compare."

Elizabeth charged at them. Ferdian had his body in front of Melanie's before she could blink. "I will not allow you to harm her."

Elizabeth spat at him. He laughed and snapped his fingers. Elizabeth grabbed her throat as her eyes widened. It was easy to see he was choking her with his power and if Melanie felt even the tiniest portion of the good Elizabeth she'd once known was there, she would have intervened. She didn't.

Ferdian glanced over his shoulder. "What shall I do with her, Melanie? You are to be the lady of the house. It is your decision to make. Do you wish for her to live?"

"No," Melanie said evenly.

Smiling, Ferdian clicked his fingers and Elizabeth went up in flames. Her screams filled the room, sinking deep into the pit of Melanie's gut. She forced her face to remain steady as Ferdian leaned over her body and stared down at her. "What shall we do now that she is out of the way?"

A flash in the corner of the room alerted Melanie that Green was there and moving. She cupped Ferdian's face and raked her gaze over him slowly. "I think we should...." Tugging on his head, she guided him towards her more.

He licked his lower lip. "You think we should what?"

"Call for reinforcements," she whispered a second before she slammed her forehead into his. Pain shot through her head but she held strong. "Daddy! Eadan!"

Ferdian was ripped free of her body by Green a second before white light flooded the room. Her father appeared as did Eadan. Both looked toward Green as he lifted Ferdian off the floor with one hand. He growled, tightening his grip on Ferdian's throat. "How dare you think you could lay a hand on my wife? The mother of my child? My mate?"

Her father glanced at her and raised an eyebrow. She nodded and he seemed to think about it for a moment before nodding his approval. Eadan just looked shocked by what was going on.

Ferdian's power surged, filling the room. Melanie, her father and brother all drew upon their magik, ready to protect Green and kill Ferdian. To their shock, Green tipped his head back and laughed.

"Think again, asshole. It's not going to work. I could have killed Elizabeth but the second I realized you'd taken Melanie, I needed her to find my wife so I let Elizabeth think she'd bested me." Green lifted his other hand and let claws erect from it. "When I 'got lucky' and bit you, your blood merged with my shifter DNA, giving me power similar to yours. Taking Melanie as my mate allowed her power to merge with mine as well."

Ferdian's eyes widened as he mouthed the word "no".

Green swept his clawed hand out, yanking his other hand away from Ferdian's neck just as his razor sharp claws made contact. In an instant, Eadan was there, cradling Melanie to his chest, blocking her view of what was transpiring. She pushed at him to move but he didn't.

"Let me go! Green! I need to see if Green's okay!"

Eadan held her tight. "He is, Mel. He's fine but not in control of himself right now. He wouldn't want you to see him like this. Come on," he wrapped his power around her, "Dad will calm him down and bring him to us."

With that, Eadan used his magik to transport the two of them back to the compound. He released her and in an instant, Peren and Missy were there, hugging her tightly.

"You're okay!" Peren began checking her over.

Missy kissed her cheek. "We were scared to death."

Lukian stepped forward. "Green?"

Eadan nodded. "Is fine. My dad is calming him down. He killed Ferdian and ... umm ... let's just say he needs to unwind a bit before he's around anyone else."

The rest of the I-Ops nodded. It was then Melanie noticed the sadness in their eyes. Since they'd just been told about Green and that he was fine, she knew it was something else. It hit her then. "Where's Wilson?"

Jon closed his eyes and turned away. Roi clasped his shoulder and squeezed it tight. "Jon, he died protecting Green's mate. The same as you would have done. It was an honorable death."

Her breath caught. Wilson was dead? No. He couldn't be. She took a tiny step back and shook her head. "No. He's not dead. No."

Missy tried to calm her but she side stepped her friend. "No. He can't be dead. I won't accept it. I'd have felt it. I shared my blood with him. A tiny piece of him is forever bonded to me. I would know."

Eadan nodded. "She's right, she would feel it if he were truly dead."

Lukian glanced at Roi and then sighed. "I understand that Fae magik is powerful but we've combed the area. His body is nowhere to be found and with the amount of blood left behind, he couldn't survive. Not with being injured to start with. From the count of rounds, they put at least fifty bullets into him." He swallowed hard and Peren wrapped her arms around him. "None of us could have survived that, Eadan."

Melanie refused to accept it, regardless what Lukian said. "He's not dead."

"Who's not dead?" Green asked from behind her.

She swung around to find Green standing side by side with her father. She rushed into his arms and hugged him, savoring how safe he made her feel. "Wilson."

Green stiffened. "Melanie, honey, he's gone. I don't know what they did with his body but I got a fairly good idea of what they did to him. He couldn't survive that."

She pressed her forehead to his sweaty chest. "You knew before you let Elizabeth capture you. You knew he was dead?"

"Yes," he said, his voice low. He held her to him and rocked her gently. "Wilson was a great man and a remarkable solider. More than that, he was like a brother to us--a brother who would sacrifice himself to save one of our mates."

"He's not dead, Green. He's not."

"Melanie, calm down. Please. You've been through enough." He slid a hand down and over her abdomen. "The baby needs you to calm down. So do I."

"Captain," Jon said. "I'd like permission to stay on for a bit even though we've collected all the Intel we came for on Krauss' compound."

Lukian was silent for a moment.

Melanie's father cleared his throat. "Since I'm sensing my son wants to stay as well and I know full well that you can't operate three men short, I'd like to volunteer to stay and help look for Wilson. I'll call Melissa's father and see to it additional men are sent down. From what I hear, you boys are in charge of stopping a mad man."

Lukian nodded. "We are but regardless of our mission, we're a family. One who won't leave another behind."

"He's dead," Roi said, his voice low, full of pain. He might have razzed Wilson but it was easy to see he loved him like a brother.

"I know but I'm still granting Jon permission to remain behind. Four weeks tops, Jon. Not a day more."

"Yes, sir," Jon said. "Thank you, sir."

Eadan stepped forward. "With your permission, sir, I'd like to stay with Jon and help...."

Lukian gave him a hard look. "You're filling in on our team, Eadan, and I have to say I want you on permanently but I know your first loyalties lie with PSI. I also know that unless you can walk on water and clone yourself, you can't be spread any thinner. Permission denied."

Chapter Fifteen

Green held Melanie, one arm draped around her as they lay in his room aboard the I-Ops private Jet. Roi and Lukian were piloting so that Green and Melanie could rest. He was positive they were hoping they'd do more than rest but Green wasn't willing to risk Melanie or the baby to sate his needs.

She rolled into him and sniffed his armpit. Laughing she pulled back and stared up at him. "I don't know about you but I'm damn happy we got to shower before boarding."

"Are you saying I smelled bad?"

"Yep. You smelled like," she bit her lower lip, "umm, death."

He put his face in her hair and inhaled, savoring her scent. "You smell wonderful, honey."

"Well, you smell better now." She smiled and kissed his lips lightly. "I'm sorry about Elizabeth. I couldn't let her live, Green, not with what she'd become."

"Shh," he said, pressing his finger to her lips. "Don't apologize. I already told you that you are my true mate. No one else. She wouldn't have wanted to live that way, Melanie. The Elizabeth I once knew would have been thankful not to be a monster. She would have been very happy for us."

Melanie tucked into his arms and he got the feeling she wasn't sure his love for her was true. Green kissed her forehead and gave her a gentle squeeze. "What are you doing in about two months?"

She hummed slightly. "Most likely, losing my waistline when I start filling out from your little one growing within me."

He liked the sound of that.

"Why?" she asked.

He wagged his brows. "I was hoping you could stop by the church of your father's choosing, so I can marry you in front of your family and our friends."

Melanie drew back and tears welled in her eyes. "What?"

"Melanie Daly-Green, will you marry me?"

She bit her trembling lower lip. "I ... I ... already mated with you, Thad. I'm already your wife."

His chest tightened. "I know. Now, I want the world to know. Okay, maybe not the world or I'd have to explain how I don't look a day over thirty-five when I'm really a hell of a lot older than that but you get the idea. So, will you?"

"I will but," she tipped her head a bit, "I want to wait until Wilson comes home. He has to be there with us."

He nodded, not wanting to get back into the debate of Wilson's death again. He was too thankful to have his wife and his unborn child safe and in his arms to spoil the moment. "That sounds perfect, honey."

A slow, sexy smile moved over her face and he caught the gleam of mischief in her eyes. When she slid her hand down his torso, Green knew what his mate wanted. She wanted him. His cock hardened and his shifter side picked up on the smell of her arousal. It spurred him onward, making his palms tingle with the urge to shift, to release power, something, anything.

I want you so much, but if I touch you, I won't be able to control myself.

He didn't voice his concern. Instead, he took hold of Melanie's wrist and brought her hand to his lips. Kissing it gently, he lowered his gaze. "Rest, honey."

I could help you control it, Thad.

He stilled. Had she really just read his mind? It wasn't a surprise when Missy and Peren began communicating with their mates mentally. They each carried shifter DNA within them.

Melanie stroked his cheek. "Did you figure it out yet, Dr. Green?"

Puzzled, his forehead crinkled.

She laughed. "You know how you gained power from our mating?"

"You licked my blood," he said, astounded that he was able to transfer some of his DNA to her. "What else can you do?"

A stain of pink covered her cheeks quickly. "Well, I can't turn into an animal but I can do this."

He watched in awe as Melanie's blue eyes swirled, intensifying. The beast within Green rose to the surface recognizing the call of its mate. He cleared his throat, trying to find the will to cage his beast.

A pounding on the door grabbed his attention. "What?" he asked hoarsely.

"Umm," Eadan's voice filtered through. "Captain wants me to pass on an order to you."

Melanie kissed Green's neck, sending his body into a frenzy. He took hold of her shoulders gently to keep her at bay as he focused on the door. "What's his order? Does he need me to pilot for a while?"

"No." It was easy to pick up on Eadan's discomfort. "He, umm, he's ordered you ... uh ... I can't say it or even think about it. Forget it."

"For the love of dick," Missy said, sounding close to the door. "Would you fuck her already, Green? The mating energy you two are letting off is wrecking havoc out here. Lukian's already threatening to put the jet on autopilot so he can have at Peren, who by the way, has locked herself in his room for fear he'll do her until she's raw."

Melanie's rich laugh warmed him. She tugged on his hand, guiding it up and under her shirt. "You heard her. Captain's orders."

"The baby," Green said, fighting to hold on to the last piece of resolve he had. "You need rest, honey."

Her rather long, tempting blink left pre-cum seeping from the tip of his cock. "Thad, the minute you ended Ferdian and my link with," she glanced away, avoiding Elizabeth's name, "*her* ended, my body stopped fighting itself. I'm strong enough to keep our child safely within me. And...."

She pushed him onto his back and straddled his waist. "You heard Lukian tell you that the Fae power within me is intensified with sex. The best way to assure I'm powerful enough is to--"

Green pulled her down and captured her lips with his. Wasting no time, he thrust his tongue in, enjoying the taste of his wife. She moaned as their tongues intertwined and he rubbed his clothed cock against her. He broke the kiss long enough to flip her onto her back and settle over her.

"I like this side of you," she said between kisses.

"What side is that?"

"The dominant one."

He held up a hand and let a claw emerge from the tip of his index finger. "Good because I'm about to cut these clothes from your body and have my way with you."

"Or," she licked his lower lip and the buzz of power surrounded him, "I could show you how to use the power you have now."

Green arched a brow. Instantly, it felt as if Melanie was reaching deep within him, yet her hands never left their spot. Something tugged within him, grabbing hold of the power that now resided within his body. Vaguely, he heard chants within his head but couldn't make out what they were saying. Suddenly, he felt his clothing disappear and the feel of Melanie's naked flesh beneath him. "What the...?"

She let out a sultry laugh. "This is how it can be between mated Fae, Thad. Now that you're technically a Fae as well, we can also tap into our power when we make love."

"It feels like your caressing me from the inside out."

Something flickered in her blue eyes and the feel of tiny bites covered his entire body. They weren't hard enough to break the skin but they were enough to excite the animal side of him.

He fought for control. "Melanie," he ground out. "I'll hurt you."

"No." She bit at his lower lip. "You'll fuck me until we both pass out, loving me the entire time. The same as I love you."

With that, he pushed her legs apart with his knee, aligned his cock and thrust to the hilt. He did exactly what she'd predicted. He fucked her with a fire that actually scared him. The need he felt for Melanie was crippling. Without her, he would die.

She wrapped her long slender legs around his waist and countered his every thrust. It was as it should be. Her pussy fisted him, holding tight, not wanting to relinquish his cock. That was fine by him. He pumped harder, losing where he stopped and she began.

Her legs quivered as she raked her nails down his back. Green knew she was coming and didn't fight the urge to do so as well. With a growl, he thrust and held himself there, filling her to the brink with his seed.

* * * *

Eadan stayed as far away from the I-Ops personal quarters as he could. Roi glanced over his shoulder and grinned. Eadan glared at him. "Dare make a joke and I'm likely to shoot you."

Lukian snorted as he continued to pilot the plane. Roi glanced at him and laughed. "Yeah, at least my wife didn't run for cover the minute she sensed mating energy."

Missy moved up and sat next to Eadan. "That's because I'm positive I could kick your ass. Peren isn't so sure she could take Lukian."

At that, Lukian lost it, laughing so hard that no sound came out. Roi slapped him in the upper arm but laughed as well. He shrugged. "Sad but true."

Missy ignored him and put her hand on Eadan's thigh. There was a time when the very thought of her touch would have left him hard and aching for release. The moment she mated with Roi, something deep within him changed. He also began to feel empty. Whatever Melanie had done with her magik had lessened that dramatically. Now Eadan was simply confused.

"You're happy for her, right?" Missy asked.

Eadan fumbled with the drink holder of the oversized leather chair he sat in and nodded. "I am. Green will protect her and love her for eternity. I'm sure of it. He seems to make her happy, so it works for me." He glanced at his ex-wife. "I'm happy for you, too."

She smiled, her brown eyes wide. "I know. I want you to be happy too, Eadan."

He patted her hand and offered a soft, genuine smile. "I know, Missy-bean."

"You're worried about Wilson, aren't you?" she asked, her voice low.

Eadan nodded. Since they'd departed, the nagging sense that Wilson really was alive and in need of help ate at him, as it did Melanie. "I don't want to get Lukian and the others riled up but I think Melanie's right."

Missy leaned in close and kept her voice low. "Peren and I agree. We're going to work on our husbands as soon as we land. I don't doubt they'll think we're nuts so I might need a favor."

"A favor?"

"PSI resources to be exact. I can coordinate a search from I-Ops second base site, near headquarters, so long as I know you'll be there to assure an agent is available to search should I find anything that needs further investigation."

He suppressed a smile. Missy was a hellcat. He should have known she and Peren would stop at nothing to assure Wilson was brought home, dead or alive. "When Melanie comes out, pull her aside and let her in on it. She's worried sick about him. I can sense it."

Missy nodded. "We're on it. In fact, Peren isn't locked away from Lukian to avoid his mating lust, she's going over maps of the area."

Eadan laughed from the gut, drawing the attention of Lukian and Roi. Missy punched his arm lightly. "Smooth."

"Hey, Roi," Eadan said, grinning. "Missy wants me to make sure your daughters are born with Fae power of sex allure. I can bestow the gift upon them. I just need to touch her stomach."

Missy choked on nothing. Roi's eyes widened and his gaze landed on Missy. For a minute, it looked as if his head might come clean off. "You want him to make our daughters give off a vibe to attract men? Are you crazy? Do you think I want men mystically attracted to them as well? That's it--I'm building a tower when we get home. Consider it the new nursery."

Winking, Eadan got up and left Missy to deal with Roi. By the time Roi was done obsessing, he'd forget everything else.

Epilogue

Two Months Later…

Wilson lifted his head as high as he could before the pain set in once more. A distant, yet constant, low-grade sound continued to be emitted from somewhere, causing his ears to feel as if they would burst. Silver-coated chains dug into his wrists and ankles, threatening to cut straight through if he dared to struggle against them much more. Even knowing the outcome, he still tugged, refusing to believe he'd spend the rest of his days locked away.

He wasn't sure how long he'd been in the small, dank cell but one thing was for sure, he didn't plan on staying much longer. Dead or alive, he would be free. Whatever they'd injected him with dulled his senses, making things blur and his body weak. At random times, he could feel the power Melanie had passed onto him trying to surface but it either wasn't sure what to do or knew he was clueless so it didn't bother lending a hand.

He swallowed, his throat dry and his body weak. The food, if it could even be called that, wasn't fit for human consumption. Maggots infested the majority of it and the rest was in a state of decomposition. After a certain point, Green had forced some of it down only to find it coming back up quickly. Still, any nourishment he could get was needed if he planned on regaining his strength and escaping.

Glancing at the small tin can, near his right hand, Wilson sighed. The water they'd brought him was brown and looked as though they'd gathered it from a mud puddle. He had little doubt they did. In shifted form, he wasn't too particular about what he ate or drank--that being said, his rat form wouldn't even eat what his captures continued to try to pawn off on him.

Closing his eyes, Wilson focused again, trying to connect with the I-Ops. It was pointless. In all the time he'd been held captive they'd not responded. Each day that passed left him weaker and weaker. Soon, he wouldn't have the strength to even try to communicate.

They'll come, his inner voice said.

Sighing, Wilson gave into fatigue, hoping beyond hopes that his instincts were right--that the I-Ops would indeed look for him.

THE END

Immortal Ops Personnel Files
TOP SECRET
Alpha Team
Name: Captain Lukian Vlakhusha

Age: Not listed. Sources say he is around a hundred and fifty years old.

Position: First-in-command, all of them just call him "Captain." Answers only to Colonel Brooks.

Call Name: Alpha Dog One.

Hair: Shoulder-length, wavy black hair.

Eyes: Royal, unnaturally blue eyes and thick, dark black lashes.

Height: 6' 3"

Distinguishing Characteristics: Tiny scar above right eyebrow, five o'clock shadow, lycanthrope (can shift into a wolf).

Additional Notes: Lukian can read human minds with ease. He is the son of the Lycan King (who has died) and his mother was human. Until he came along, the bloodline in his family was pure lycan. He is King now though he does not fulfill his duties. Lukian, as well as all of the other I-Ops, has been repeatedly offered higher ranks. He, like the others, refuse, not seeing the reasoning for it.

Relation to Any of the Other Team Members: Yes. Lukian's DNA was used to create Roi. He is his brother by way of genetic alteration now. They are also best friends.

Mission Report Devoted to Him: *Immortal Ops: Book I*-- Captain Lukian Vlakhusha is having issues with his newest target, Peren Matthews. Something about her has left him staring at her picture and wondering what it would be like to touch her soft skin. When the time comes for the team to strike, Lukian senses danger and aborts the mission. He makes an attempt at meeting Peren and is set in his place by the independent young woman who knows what she is and isn't looking for in a man. Lukian is having trouble telling Peren that he's what she fears most: a werewolf. Can they make the passion that burns between them last, or will Lukian's condition be too much for Peren?

~~*****~~

Name: Major Geoffroi (Roi) Majors
Age: Not listed. Sources say he is over fifty.

Position: Second in command.
Call Name: Alpha Dog Two
Hair: Shoulder-length, black hair
Eyes: Royal, unnaturally blue eyes
Height: 6' 4"
Distinguishing characteristics: Stubble-covered jaw line; lycanthrope (can shift into a wolf); was genetically altered

Additional Notes: Bad attitude; convinced he is a ladies man. Does not deal well with authority and has been known to tell Colonel Brooks to go fuck himself.

Relation to Any of the Other Team Members: Yes. Lukian's DNA was used to create him. He is his brother by way of genetic alteration now. They are also best friends.

Mission Report Devoted to Him: *Immortal Ops: Book II-- Critical Intelligence*--Missy Carter leads a boring, overworked life as a system analyst for the State Department or rather, that's what she lets everyone believe. In reality, her life is anything but boring. As an agent with Paranormal Security and Intelligence (PSI), she's seen and done it all. Intelligence is her specialty, assassination is her hobby. The only problem is that the things she spies on don't die easily. She's learned to handle anything life can throw at her. That is until the biggest paramilitary pain in her ass shows up ... again. Lucky for him, he's sexy.

Roi Majors, second-in-command of the I-Ops, is having a hard time believing that Intel can only get half the information needed to bring down an underground ring of vampires who are hell bent on creating a race of supernaturals with multiple strands of DNA. As the team looks for answers, Roi searches for sexual release. When he's paired with the one woman in the world who seems immune to his self-proclaimed charms, he can't wait to see her to safety and bid her good riddance. He never counted on falling in love with her. And he sure as hell never counted on her claiming to be an agent with a branch of the government no *human* should know about.

~~* * * * *~~

Name: Eadan Daly
Age: 30 years old.
Position: PSI- Paranormal Security and Intelligence- Shadow Operative, answers to Director of PSI-- General

Jack Newman; filling in at I-Ops until a suitable replacement can be found, currently pulling dual duty.

Call Name: Alpha Dog Three.

Hair: Long silky blond hair.

Eyes: Blue-gray eyes.

Height: 6' 5"

Distinguishing Characteristics: Baby face, tall, toned, Fae with magikal abilities.

Additional Notes: He was Melissa "Missy" Carter's handler for nine years. He was also married to her. They lost a child. His sister is Melanie Daly. Has an affinity for 80's music; served with PSI for over ten years now.

Relation to Any of the Other Team Members: No.

Mission Report Devoted To Him: Classified.

Bravo Team

Name: Doctor Thaddeus Chandler Green

Age: Not listed. Sources say he is at least one hundred.

Position: Bravo Team Leader.

Call Name: Bravo Dog One.

Hair: Close-cut red hair, so dark it borders on brown.

Eyes: Emerald

Height: 6' 4"

Distinguishing Characteristics: Muscle bound, were-panther, survived an attack in lab while working as a scientist. Was not genetically altered but rather infected by an escaping were-panther.

Additional Notes: Genius, handles all of the I-Ops medical and the majority of their technical needs. Also heavily involved in genetic research. His wife died fifty years ago while trying to give birth to their son, who also died. It was then the I-Ops learned they cannot reproduce with human women. Can "sense truths"-- similar to a vampire's skills. For the most part, is a gentle giant.

Relation to Any of the Other Team Members: Yes. Green's DNA was used to create Lance--his brother by way of genetic alteration.

Mission Report Devoted to Him: *Immortal Ops: Book III--Radar Deception*

~~* * * * *~~

Name: Jonathon "Jon" Reynell

Age: Not listed. Sources say he is at least fifty.

Position: Sniper--accurate within 4000 meters.

Call Name: Bravo Dog Two (but is often called "Bravo Tiger Two" as joke by other I-Ops).
Hair: Close-cut blond hair.
Eyes: Amber.
Height: 6' 1"
Distinguishing Characteristics: Looks about twenty-five years old. Is a were-tiger. Excellent eyesight.
Additional Notes: Has a southern drawl, asks his "momma' for forgiveness as he snipes. Polite. Harbors something dark that he hasn't shared with his team members. Prone to motion sickness.
Relation to Any of the Other Team Members: No. Had been genetically altered with the intent to make Wilson his brother by way of genetics but an accidental mix up occurred, preventing that.
Mission Report Devoted to Him: Classified.

~~* * * * *~~

Name: Wilson Rousseau
Age: Not listed. Sources say he is at least fifty.
Position: Rifleman and demolitions expert.
Call name: Bravo Dog Three (but is often called "Bravo Rat Three" as joke by other I-Ops).
Hair: Shaggy dark brown with slightest hint of gold, natural highlights in it.
Eyes: Chocolate brown.
Height: 6' 2"
Distinguishing Characteristics: Were-rat, who is accidentally exposed to various strands of genetically-altered DNA, among other things.
Additional Notes: Team smartass. Doesn't mind being butt of jokes to keep up morale. Has a heart of gold.
Relation to Any of the Other Team Members: No. Intended to be Jon's brother by way of genetics but an accidental mix up occurred, preventing that.
Mission Report Devoted to Him: Classified.

Excerpt from WARRIORS OF THE DARKNESS by Mandy M. Roth, now available in ebook and tradepaper from New Concept Publishing.
© copyright March 2006, Mandy M. Roth

Chapter One

Colonel Alejandro Vargas watched silently, ready and willing to shoot Lt. Fulk Rodriquez if he dared to cross the line with the two civilian doctors that were assigned until further notice to their team. Rodriquez would heal the wound--eventually. It's what their kind did. Some shifters took longer than others but in the end, he'd be just fine.

"So, what's that say?" Fulk asked, tapping the wall full of carvings with his M-16. It was the last thing he should do in a place as old as the temple they'd found but it was so typical of Fulk that no one commented, not even the attractive doctor that had been working so hard to decipher the writing. She seemed to be in a world all her own, the same as her counterpart who had not ventured from her post either.

Both women were more than attractive, though one had managed to not only capture his attention but seemed to demand it. Dr. Murray's golden waves of hair touched her mid-back and her blue eyes continued to flicker in his direction from time to time. Her body was so close to perfect that he had a hard time believing no part of it was altered. At five feet ten inches tall she came to his chin and that was a rare find. From what he could gather by staring at her, her army issued desert fatigues and dark tan tee shirt did little to hide a toned and well curved body. His cock liked what it saw, so the rest of him wasn't about to complain.

Alejandro couldn't tell if Dr. Murray was interested in him or nervous of him. Each time he caught her watching him, she looked away quickly. It was kind of cute and left him feeling young again. He was dressed in fatigues and packing enough ammunition and weapons to take out a small army so it was understandable if it was the latter of the two. He knew he looked intimidating. Any other time, he'd have been pleased to think he was making someone nervous but the idea of scaring her sickened him.

Dr. Ondrea Harris, the petite friend of the blonde one stood slowly and ran her fingers over the markings on the wall. "They're based loosely off Egyptian hieroglyphics but they aren't like anything I've ever seen before. It's freaky."

Freaky? Great, this is one of our experts.

Fulk nodded, his chin length brown hair fell into his face. "This whole place is freaky. One minute we're standing in a desert and the next we're in a tropical rainforest. I keep waiting for a snowstorm to hit. This sure the hell isn't like our Earth."

She smiled. "I agree. From the base to here we spent less than fifteen minutes driving and covered that much of a climate and terrain change. It's remarkable.

"I just can't understand how it is that they have Egyptian writing here as well. From all outward appearances, this temple looks Mayan, yet, I'm positive these aren't Mayan markings. The strangest part of it all is that I'm sure some of this is Latin as well. I've never seen anything like it." Ondrea glanced towards her friend who was busy with her nose in a pile of books. "Dr. Murray, come take a look at this."

The blonde goddess continued to fiddle near a pedestal with her electronic equipment and books. She hummed softly and moved her alluring hips to music only she heard. It was both erotic and endearing. It seemed as though she didn't have a care in the world. She'd arrived early in the morning and never once appeared shocked by the idea of being on a different planet or in another realm--whatever the scientist of the week was calling it. It was as though she did it daily. Maybe she did. Alejandro had requested files on all personnel coming aboard the project and was given all but hers. So far, he didn't even know her first name and hadn't heard her utter much more than a thank you. Granted, that one thank you had left his entire body cramping with the need to sink his dick into her.

He was sure of one thing, her smile made him weak in the knees. Already, she'd flashed her pearly whites at him twice, each time leaving his stomach flip-flopping and his heart racing. Alejandro felt like a love-struck junior high student. It was oddly liberating and terrifying all at the same time. There was also something familiar about her, but the idea of forgetting a face like hers was absurd, so he dismissed it.

Ondrea snorted. "Hello? Dr. Murray? Anyone home there or are you too busy locked up in your world of science to come back to us?"

The blonde kept swaying her hips while she held a pen in her mouth. Alejandro never before wanted to be a ballpoint pen. He did now. She tapped keys on her laptop and glanced at a stack of papers to her right. "Hmm."

Ondrea smiled. "Hello, paging Dr. Murray. Is there a Dr. Murray in the freaky realm?"

Fulk chuckled. Dr. Murray danced in a small circle before returning to whatever it was that had been holding her attention all morning. Ondrea cast him a sideways glance. "Erm, I'd apologize for her but, really, she'll only keep doing it. Plus, I'm one hundred percent sure that she has no idea she's even doing it. She just sort of shuts off to everything around her when she gets going with something she's into."

Biting his lower lip, Alejandro did his best not to laugh at Dr. Murray as she tucked the pen behind her ear, picked up a piece of paper and danced while reading it. The worst part of it all was that not only was it funny to see a scientist not having a care in the world, it made him horny as hell to watch this one in particular.

Fulk grabbed a piece of native fruit from a tree near him and went to crack its outer shell. "I'm starved. I've got to admit these aren't so bad. Taste a little like a pear mixed with an apple. Weird, but good."

Ondrea glanced at him. "Hand me one."

He gave her an odd look.

She rolled her eyes. "Please."

Grinning, Fulk tossed a piece of what they'd taken to calling monkey-nuts because it was their job to go out of their way to be men and think of names for things to offend others. That and the monkey-like creatures that seemed to inhabit this particular section of the jungle seemed to like not only eating them but throwing them at the soldiers.

Ondrea caught the fruit and stared at Dr. Murray. A slow smile slid over her face. It was mischievous to say the least.

"You are not going to throw that at her," Alejandro said, before he even thought about it.

Ondrea winked. "Wow, a little overprotective, aren't you?"

Yes, but that wasn't the point. Alejandro shrugged. "No. I'd just rather not have to explain why I let one civilian doctor knock another out. That's all."

"She'll live. It's fruit."

"With a spiked outer shell," he said, giving her a hard look.

Alejandro could almost see the wheels in Ondrea's head spinning. Oh, she was going to throw it at Dr. Murray now just because he'd told her not to. He watched in what felt like slow motion as Ondrea hurled the fruit at Dr. Murray who was still dancing and reading from a piece of paper. The fruit had aligned perfectly with her head.

Drawing his bowie knife from its sheath, he sent it flying, ax-like at the fruit. It struck it, as he knew it would and changed the direction of the fruit. The knife wedged into a purple tree trunk to the right of Dr. Murray, spearing the fruit in the process.

Ondrea clapped. "Nice. But it wouldn't have hurt her. Just so you know."

Dr. Murray glanced at the tree and reached out tentatively. Taking hold of the handle, she pulled the knife free from the tree. She turned and arched a brow, appearing to be a little lost as to what was going on. "Did someone call me?"

Alejandro bit back a laugh as he held his M-16 close to him, needing anything to keep his mind off sinking his cock into her. The very idea of being able to touch her, caress her while he slid into what could only be a tight pussy made his palms begin to sweat and his stomach tighten. She would be the death of him if he had to stand around staring at her shaking her ass every day.

Each time she hummed, Alejandro pictured that lush mouth wrapped around his shaft, taking him deep into the back of her throat. The very thought of it left him on the verge of coming. Reaching down, he did a slight adjusting of his rock hard cock, hoping she wouldn't notice.

She's probably married. Nothing that fine can possibly be available. Besides, my family would have a fit.

Bringing a blonde-haired, blue-eyed, girl home with him for a weekend would lead to his mother casting some sort of spell over him that would no doubt leave him impotent. Since she did possess the gift of magik, it was a very real threat. All she claimed to want out of life was for her children to settle down, have lots of babies and stay close to her. Somehow he didn't think she'd be okay with a blue-eyed grandbaby. She was a proud Brazilian woman, but Alejandro guessed she'd be willing to make an exception as to what South American country his future mate originated from, only that she did indeed have ties to one and was nothing like Dr. Murray.

Staring at Dr. Murray, he doubted very much that she had ties to anything remotely close to him. It was a shame. She made his blood pump fast and his entire body light with need at the mere whiff of her scent. Fresh berries and cream seemed to permeate from her every time she moved. It drove him mad with lust so much so that he'd found himself taking the outer perimeter watch three times already since they'd arrived--each time to give himself a much needed break or risk pinning her to the ground and claiming her.

Stop thinking about her as mate material. She's human and you aren't looking to be tied down to any one woman. Now, a few nights of pleasure are another story. That is a definite possibility.

Alejandro watched as she put on the army DCU hat that he'd given her when he saw her nose and cheeks burning from the scorching sun. The soft smile she'd given in return had left his muscles tightening as he fought the urge to bend and capture her mouth. It would have been so easy to just press his lips to hers but she hadn't shown an interest in him as of yet and stealing a kiss wasn't what he did. Though, if he had to be forced to endure much more of her swaying hips and smooth looking skin, he just might. Maybe, he'd get lucky and she'd be willing to share so much more than just a kiss with him.

She made her way towards Ondrea and paused before him. "I think this is yours," she said, handing him his knife with the fruit still attached to it. "Thank you."

Did she know?

She arched a brow and glanced at her friend. "Be careful. Foreign objects seem to fall from the sky."

Ondrea whistled and glanced upwards. "No clue what you're talking about."

"Right. Thanks again, Colonel."

Printed in the United States
77318LV00001BA/133